I0734730

Cindy M. Amos

REDEEMING RIVER RANCHER
By Cindy M. Amos

The Lord says,
"Behold, I will extend to my people peace like a river,
and in its current they will claim a good life."
Isaiah 66:12

Dedicated to The Amos family
Who taught me the importance of keeping
corner posts in place
& the fine art of clipping up a barbed wire fence

The author would like to acknowledge the following
for their support and encouragement with this book:
Members of the Jane's Gang book club from WEFC
Sharon J. Amos for cover photograph
Diana Grabau, Editor www.seizethedayedits.com
Members of South Central Kansas ACFW Chapter
Literary Agent Mary Sue Seymour, for the workshop
that birthed this plot
Cynthia Hickey of Forget Me Not Romances
& Inspiration of the Holy Spirit

LANDSCAPES OF MERCY SERIES BOOK ONE
Yet there is one ray of hope:
God's compassion never ends.
Only the Lord's mercies have kept us
from complete destruction.
Great is His faithfulness;
His lovingkindness renews each day.
Lamentations 3:21-23

Chapter 1

Cavorting around the foreclosure property crossed a few lines in the bank's discourse on protocol but it sure kept the heat wave birthed by the first of June at bay. Tired of waiting for the delinquent occupant, Lacey Woodhouse bent over the rim of a livestock trough behind the tidy farmhouse doomed by mortgage non-payment. What started as splashed handfuls of water on her face soon made her wish for a good old Baptist immersion. At least the day's ninety degree temperature became much more manageable. Now if only the ranch's missing owner would return to face the music, she could get on with her life. A baby goat escaped the corral and scampered by. Interested in the cute little devil, she enticed it closer with wiggly fingers. She sighed, hopeful to get the notice served and wash her hands of another bank loan gone bad.

A blur of motion under the sheltering elm caught her eye and as she turned, the baby goat bleated behind her. A sharp bark protested the escapee and she drew a quick breath as a black and white dog darted toward her, teeth bared for business. The baby goat mistook her for a safe haven, bringing the wrath of the canine upon them both. Knocked off balance, her high heels went airborne and she fell over the trough rim. Coolness enveloped her as she fought the urge to flail against the metal tank. The barked protest gave way to an onslaught of bubbles as the trough took full possession of her assets.

~

Wray Benson knew he had company. The sleek red sports car out front had been hard to miss. While the show of watering her face had been a momentary feast for his unaccustomed eyes, it came as prelude to the drenching he now received. The wake rippled over the tank's rim along its full length before he could lift her out. Though a breathless beauty emerged, her arms protested in warrior mode as he walked her over to a dry perch beneath the elm, red shoes and all. Grandpa would have dubbed her madder than a wet hen, as her brow furrowed in displeasure above a pair of emerald green eyes that shot sparks. Wetness soon soaked into his senses, which leaked down his chest in a pleasurable sop.

At least his arms worked now, as other once-loyal body parts seemed to be falling under house arrest with her in tight proximity. She gave a kick of protest and somehow managed to slip from his grip above the wooden bench where she landed with an ungracious plop. He straightened and backed away, which ended the physical wrangle. But that sure didn't account for the pounding of his heartbeat underneath the wetness of his cotton shirt. Wray stood over a hornet's nest of female trespass—and he kind of liked it.

~

"Of all the nerve," Lacey fumed under her breath. She swiped her wet hair back so it wouldn't interfere with her tirade. A look down at her outfit led to a gasp. She needed to recover and make her presentation of the bank notice, but see-through clothes now forfeited her professional edge. Even worse, the cowboy gawker seemed to be enjoying the view, which started another heat wave up her neck. She crossed her arms to hide her transparency.

He gave a chuckle as he stood there in the shade sizing her up. "You didn't want me to leave you in there, did you?" His mouth eased to a lopsided grin. "Maybe you need a minute alone—I could wait on the front porch."

The way out of her predicament hid from view, as if the water had washed all her purpose away, leaving only a wet bank rep floundering in front of a somewhat attractive but highly unsuccessful rancher. The good humor reflected in his eyes made her attempt to subdue her caustic attitude, lest any of this get back to the bank and put her in an unfavorable light. "That would be great."

He nodded and whistled for the dog, then tipped his hat and disappeared with long strides toward the front of the house. She turned her face skyward, breathing a prayer to help redeem her situation as she wiped the excess moisture from her face. A breeze trickled sunlight between the tree's leaves and cooled her wet skin. The sun could be her ally if she stood out in its grasp and allowed it to dry her acetate blouse back to opaque ivory again. But no hope existed for red patent leather so her shoes lasted a full two seconds before she kicked them off.

High heels in hand, she headed away from the gate toward the orchard side of the yard. For the first time, she could make out tiny fruit tucked within the branches of the closest trees. It brought her an odd delight, as though she could see a promise of sorts being borne on the limbs. She raised her arms and flapped her shirttail to aid the late afternoon wind. When a curtain moved in the rear window of the farmhouse, her private drying cycle shattered.

~

At his bedroom window, Wray watched the stranger stomp around in the wind and somehow knew trouble lurked near at hand. The black briefcase he'd spotted on the front porch swing nagged at his thoughts. One hand clutched a clean chambray shirt while the other one held the curtain back so he could get a better view. He stood a man divided—and now he couldn't even trust his own eyes. Only when she disappeared into the side yard could he pull himself away and do what he'd intended from the start.

He walked through the hallway and found Hank had fallen into step to join him in the adventure. Whatever came next, there wasn't any reason he couldn't have his loyal canine with him. Maybe it would even loosen things up for them, although the animal approach had not worked its charm so far. A worry dug at him but he dodged it by stepping into the kitchen where he prepared two glasses of ice water.

Contained liquid shouldn't be a problem on a hot summer's day. He tucked one glass under his elbow as he pulled the front door open.

At the passenger side of her car, she stood clamping a clip into her limp black hair. Still wet, he diverted his gaze down at the lawn instead of taking a cheap thrill at her predicament. The high heel shoes sat drying on the bottom step of the front porch. He placed the glasses on the base of the column and stepped down to offer her the over-shirt. When he cleared his throat, she glanced back and seemed to assess her options without a word, then snatched the chambray cover from his hand and motioned him away.

As he retreated to his own porch, a rare smile dug into his cheek, the effect somewhat enjoyable. This encounter would prove to be interesting, to say the very least. He claimed his glass and headed for the porch swing but the ominous black briefcase deflected his intent. Instead, he brought a wooden chair up from the other side. From there she could state her business and he'd play captive audience, despite all the warning signs.

~

Lacey had her banker hat back on and could pull off this much-delayed notification before she disappeared into the sunset with her dignity still intact. She turned and stomped barefoot up the front steps. Without making eye contact, she targeted the briefcase and dug out the portfolio containing the River Ranch file. The paperwork somehow lent her power, as considerable preparation had gotten her this far. It would serve both parties fairly if she rendered it straight up.

"I'm Lacey Woodhouse from Fidelis Bank." She paused and allowed the words to sink in before continuing. His gaze fell a bit at the recognition of the bank's name but to his credit, he did not react in knee-jerk anger like many other clients had done. She read that as a sign she could proceed, so she produced a letter for his attention. "First, let me make sure that I'm speaking to Wraylon D. Benton." The dog joined them on the front porch and dropped at the feet of its master as though to make the verification unnecessary.

"Yes, you are, but you can call me Wray for short," he replied in a matter-of-fact manner. "My father went by Wraylon, so I answer to the nickname. And this is Hank, my dog."

"Very well, Wray." She kept her tone all business. "Since you are fully aware that your mortgage payments have gone unpaid for the last six months, we—as your lender—hereby place you under this Notice of Default." She handed him the letter. His penetrating gaze landed as a direct hit on her sensitivity. She chided herself for not having her defense shield already leveled in place as a Teflon-coated bank representative. From now on she would have to be more careful.

He took a long drink of water and she allowed him time to read the letter top to bottom so he could appreciate the full gravity of his financial situation. She paced back toward the porch swing but decided not to sit in it as an endorsement of coziness. Foreclosure represented serious business.

"What's next?" He glanced over at her for more information.

Lacey pretended to check her notes, although she

knew the process by heart. Neither of them would benefit by a mistake at this juncture, so better to keep it slow and accurate than rush through just so she could get away from here. "With this Notice of Default, we now put you—the borrower—on notice that you face foreclosure on the property identified in the letter, commonly referred to in the memo line as 'River Ranch.'"

"Just for clarification," he interjected, "the borrower was my father, not me. I inherited the loan debt when the farm came to me three years ago as his heir." He flounced the letter in his hand and held her gaze with expectancy.

Lacey nodded at his concession, which broke her rhythm. "With my delivery of this letter, a clock now begins to tick defining a timeframe during which you may respond to save your property." Her voice wobbled and she stopped to swallow. What in the world was happening to her? She had set forth this spiel at least ten times in the last month, so how could it be that she had acquired any newfound sympathy today? When she glanced back up he stood close, handing her a glass of water. She accepted and drank out of instinctive need. She offered a slight smile of appeasement as he sat and shot her a concerned look.

Distracted by a faint scar on his chin, she inhaled, and a stitch knotted under her ribs. "Listen very carefully. If the default is not corrected within three months, I will meet with you to establish a foreclosure sale date. However, you will have a reinstatement period that runs from today until five days before the auction. Sometimes we call this the redemption period, and only after it expires can the next stage begin."

"I don't plan to let it go that far, ma'am." Wray folded the letter in half.

"Most folks have good intentions Mr. Benson, but I want you to be aware of the sequence—so there aren't any surprises. The sheriff's eviction comes next. He'll visit with the order to evict and come back a few days later to make sure it happens. Once the bank files that motion to evict, it is impossible to get more time to stay in the house. The property will sell on the courthouse steps to the highest bidder who must pay cash to receive the trustee's deed."

"Again, I don't plan to let it go that far," he repeated. "River Ranch will not be forfeited to foreclosure, I assure you, Miss Woodhouse. Let me thank the Fidelis Bank for their forbearance up until this point. I will come by well within the redemption period and bring the funds necessary to halt this process. I have no intention of losing two generations of hard work to my father's farm equipment loan that was ill-advised from the get-go."

"And I applaud you for that in terms of your latent valor," Lacey replied in sincerity. "But in this case, money represents the better part of valor and is the only thing that will halt the process. As the official representative of Fidelis Bank, I hereby place you on Notice of Default, which must be corrected within ninety days. Three months, Mr. Benson. Is that clear?"

Her defaulting loan client seemed to be lost in his own thoughts as she crossed the porch to leave. She unbuttoned the chambray shirt and let it drop on his thigh as she walked by, her laden briefcase weighing every footfall. The Border collie lifted its head and whined as she passed, which poked her heart with unexpected sentimentality.

As she descended the steps, she maneuvered around to the driver's side of her car. Without ceremony, she pitched the briefcase into the rear floorboard. Something seemed left undone, but for the life of her, she couldn't figure out what. She scanned the façade of the cottage once more and pulled her car door open to enter. A motion on the porch snagged her attention. As she slid her protective sunglasses in place on the bridge of her nose, she regarded the rancher.

His arm swept across the impressive farmyard vista. "I appreciate you coming all the way out to River Ranch."

When a faint smile followed the comment, she stared over the top of her glasses to better judge his sincerity. Although no words came to her rescue, her head gave a slight nod without cerebral consent. Heat flooded up her neck again, so she ducked for cover. She cranked the ignition to make a hasty get-away. Unfortunately, he'd planted his truck well within her turning radius and she had to back around to pull out and regain access to the road.

The interior steaming hot, she pressed the windows down as she hit reverse and let the car back up in aversion to the truck. She forced the steering wheel into correction of her dilemma and eased into forward gear but soon found the mailbox too close for comfort. This time when she rectified her angle of departure, she found him poised right outside her window, her red high heels dangling from his fingers like poison.

"I won't be needing these." His lips tightened to control his enjoyment of her predicament but the mirth shown in his eyes.

She lowered the window all the way and grabbed the errant shoes.

"You might want to consider wearing some lower heels if you make a habit of poking around the countryside." He drawled out the last few words for emphasis. This time his grin couldn't be restrained, so ample it pulled at the chin scar. "And now you know where I am."

Her cheeks burned as more than her blouse appeared to be see-through, but something about the sincerity in his eyes held her back from stomping the accelerator. She put her bank hat back on instead. "Mr. Benson, I hope I don't have to come out here again, as we'll be setting the auction date for dispossession if I do." A dazed feeling rendered her quick mind inert as his expression seemed to warm. He must have misunderstood her response.

"Come back and I'll take you down to the river." His blue eyes disappeared beneath the rim of his hat as he backed away.

She eased up on the clutch to let the high performance engine rip her from the countryside and his intense gaze. The wild daisies waved farewell from the pasture as she barreled under the arching wrought iron sign labeling River Ranch. Before she knew it, the road's washboard finish returned under her low-slung car. The drive back to town became a series of bone-jarring jolts. This time when she made the river crossing, she slowed to peer over the railing to see what the water looked like down below.

Chapter 2

Lacey took in the chaos of the early morning buzz of yard sale shoppers around the tranquil village of Maize and braced for the onslaught of her partner's purchasing prowess. A car lock beeped behind her as she lost her visual momentum to a guy bench-pressing a metal rod ringed with multiple weights. Another man cheered each repetition up by the garage.

"We'll skip this one—it's all guy stuff." Julie caught up beside her. "Though I must admit, the testosterone display over there is a bonus. I'm here to slay the day in the purchasing department, so don't let me get sidetracked by an overzealous man."

"Heaven forbid," she replied, unable to subdue the laughable snort that came with the sarcasm. They walked the length of a shady yard whose owners had elected not to participate in the day's madness. Another group of women headed in their direction, prompting Julie to wing her in the ribs. She detoured across the tranquil yard to arrive first at the promising cache of household goods displayed by the neighbors. While she fixed her attention on a pair of lamps, Julie went into hone-and-hover mode as she scoured the driveway for worthy treasures.

Always in search of raw materials for her next stained glass project, Lacey evaluated the base of the lamps. She appreciated the uneven salt glaze that gave the ceramic squares an iridescent sheen. The olive green surface dimpled with a bead of milky glaze on occasion, yielding a luminous effect that would add to her artwork. An expanse of grass dotted with wildflowers came to mind and she began to weave the olive color chips into a meadow scene. Her creative juices on full flow, she touched the flat base about the time a group of shoppers wandered over. A woman picked up a mismatched set of coasters on the table's end and shot her a keep-away look.

Julie stood hunched over a crate of miscellaneous clutter down by the curb, as far away from being helpful as possible. The owner clinched a sale by the front porch and took the money, stuffing it in his pocket. She lifted a hand to gain his attention, but another woman called out at the same time. He departed to the depths of the front yard.

The coaster woman strayed closer, and in her peripheral vision, Lacey saw her regard the lampshades. When she surveyed the rickety set-up of wooden plank shelving elevated by empty Mason jars, she grew unsure whether she could pluck both lamps off their perch and wrestle them to the check-out area. A dog bark tore the placid morning, and she looked over in time to see Julie startle and throw a handful of books into the air. Score one for the Saint Bernard, but she couldn't leave her precious lamps. The woman dared to touch the shade of the far lamp, prompting her to retaliate.

"I plan to purchase these lamps," she said, a touch more defiant than necessary. The older woman cocked her brow as though to object, only to be snuffed out by a whimpering female who had gone a little nutty down by the curb. When she looked back, Julie lay pinned under the giant canine as it licked the mocha gourmet coffee off her lips. Like a good friend, Lacey froze.

~

"If we put the tiller down by the curb, it might grab someone's attention as they drive by." Wray maneuvered the bulky piece of equipment into position. "Thanks for hosting it at your sale, Gary, as I don't get much traffic out my way."

"Maybe we should think about a trade if it doesn't sell," he said. "The way you worked those weights out, they could readily go home with you."

"A rancher has to stay fit," he replied. A woman's cry for help pierced the neighborhood and before he could evaluate it, he ran toward the source. An affable brown and white Saint Bernard pounced on a breakable thin woman two houses down and proceeded to turn the encounter into a one-sided love romp. In seconds, he laid a shoulder into the lug and its owner managed to retract the leash and haul it into the street. A wide-eyed woman succumbed to his assistance and soon found her feet. The sound of shattering glass called from up the driveway and he spotted a rickety display table wobble toward collapse.

He ran up the pavement, jumped the jagged bottom of a Mason jar, and managed to get a hand on a heavy-based lamp inches from concrete disaster. The wooden shelving gave way as a shopper screeched and the twin lamp showered down past his left hip. In swift reaction, he made contact with his boot heel and kicked the falling object toward a grass landing. It hit with a thud and the interested shopper scrambled to reconnect. Unimpressed with his heroic rescue, the shelving continued to disintegrate, which sent glass jars rolling down the driveway in errant escape. A heavy-set woman tried to outmaneuver the rolling glass but couldn't keep up to save her life. He laughed when the owner finally drew the woman aside in absolution of further responsibility for the display disaster.

Someone moved up behind him. "I'll take that lamp off your hands."

Wray turned and the sight of her sent the electric buzz of recollection down his length. Dark hair, perky up-turned nose, and fiery green eyes all came back to him as the foreclosure notification flitted through his mind. "Miss Woodhouse?" He started to relinquish the lamp, then realized it gave him more leverage to hold it back. Her jaw worked through her discomfort as the dog-attack lady joined her. He felt like a museum piece, their scrutiny sat so heavy. "Guess you could say that, once again, I have my hands full of something that belongs to you."

"Well not yet," she replied, her voice quivering. "But I'd like to buy it. Sorry I couldn't get down there to your predicament, Julie. Things got a little complicated up here."

"As it turns out, I had a better offer up off of the ground—one with muscles and not afraid to use them," Julie replied with a flirtatious wink.

Wray laughed and extended the lamp toward the flustered banker when the heavy-set woman shoved her way past Julie and reached for the lampshade.

"I just bought both these lampshades for twenty dollars," she said. The owner came up nodding and waving the bill to prove it as a gasp escaped the wannabe owner.

"In all fairness, I believe Miss Woodhouse has designs on these lamps, ma'am," Wray replied, his gaze fixed on the man. "I don't think I just rescued these from annihilation to hand them over to the first paying customer."

"Thank you, Mr. Benson." Lacey stepped closer to the lamp he held.

"Call me Wray, please." He shifted his gaze to accommodate her gracious attention.

"Okay, Wray. I apologize for the horrendous mess I've made here in the driveway and I do want the lamps, but maybe a compromise is in order. I only want the bases for the glass, so she can have the lampshades and I'll pay the balance for the rest. Does that suit everyone?"

"The glass?" he asked, not comprehending. The heavy lady unscrewed the pineapple finial on top of the lamp and shucked the shade before he could get her figured out. He held a hand out for the pineapple and she relinquished it with a harrumph.

"I plan to break it up and use it for a craft project." Lacey lowered her lamp to the beggar woman. The second shade exited much like the first and the woman departed with the homeowner. Julie giggled and slapped her petite hand over her mouth.

He tried to relax his expression to cut her source of

sidewalk entertainment. "Break it up? The glass I just saved from shattering?"

"I … I do stained glass work. I'll reframe the material into secondary use and make it beautiful in the process." Lacey fit the finial back in place.

When her expression softened, he sensed an ounce of vulnerability. The afterburner of his power rescue unraveled and his advocacy seemed misplaced. He fought the acrid urge to respond in harshness, but a biting insinuation came to mind. "So that's how it is. You're good at breaking things apart. Must come with the territory, Miss Woodhouse. Here's your lamp." He nodded to Julie and strode across the neighbor's yard to regain friendly territory. A faint "thanks" followed him, but barely penetrated his downtrodden composure. He reasoned nice-to-look-at didn't always equate to enjoyable-to-be-around, and his impulsive interest in the green-eyed banker took a nosedive. Equipment was more his speed anyway, even if he had poised himself for a break-up in that department. He passed the tiller, still ticked off at the haughty banker. He tried not to relate the two, but the twin association festered like an ill-brokered lose-lose deal.

~

"I simply have to have it." Julie ran her glossy pink fingertips over the tapestry section of the oversized ottoman. "Tell me, do you think it will match the brown of my leather sofa?"

Lacey glanced at the cottage-sized house and couldn't figure out how it had birthed such a rotund monstrosity. She squeezed her eyes closed and opened them in an attempt to gain perspective but the lump of tobacco-spit brown remained the same. "You have more of an eye for mix-and-match than I do, Julie. Go with your instincts, but I'm telling you, it's going to be a vicious space hog in your condo."

"So, I'll rearrange. I've been meaning to anyway. Now watch me barter my way down from the eighty-five dollar price tag."

"Oh, no. Spare me this scene. I've already had enough friction for one day. How about you give me the keys and let me bring your car up the street?" She held out an insistent hand and Julie complied with a tug at her shirttail.

"No loitering at the hunk station," Julie teased.

"Nothing could be further from my realm of possibilities, so don't even mention it. Talk about men being from Mars."

"No. Martians have those noodle-like little arms, not the fortress of brute strength that man carries around."

"For the record, he's the foreclosure at River Ranch, Julie. That puts him in hands-off territory even if I had been impressed. Be right back with the car." She gave a wave and jogged away. She enjoyed a brief respite in the shade that often accompanies old village lanes. As she approached the car, she released the door locks. Up the driveway metal weights clinked until the user splayed out between reps. His hands dropped to the pavement and an unexpected tinge of regret filled her chest. Did she owe him an apology just because he couldn't understand her creative process? She plopped into the driver's seat and managed to get her long legs under the wheel. An act of charity, the car soon rolled away from the man-sale and she came abreast of Julie's treasure strike before she knew it.

An age-bent man approached the car with a tape measure and she triggered the trunk release for his assessment. Julie stood by her conquest in the driveway with a defiant look that spoke to her negotiation prowess. Lacey exited the car ready to lend a hand to get the monster contained for transport.

"It ain't gonna fit in here." The measuring tape snapped back in place as the man stood puzzled at the revelation.

She shrugged at Julie who had one finger on her chin. "Can you call Gerald?" Lacey knew Julie's latest man-friend would be more than helpful in his fancy SUV.

"He's in Eastborough today at his mother's. That's a no-desecration zone, I'm afraid. What about your River Rancher friend? He's close at hand. Does he have a truck?"

"Gracious, Julie. What are you asking—for him to follow you home just to haul this?" A lump formed in her throat at the prospect, and the prod of needing to ask forgiveness resurfaced.

"Don't make it sound so mercenary, for heaven's sake. I could call in lunch and offer to feed him, since it's pushing noon. I don't think he'd take gas money even if I offered it. He looks as honest as the day is long, so I don't understand what your objection is." Julie shooed the homeowner away as another group of shoppers appeared up the drive.

"The lamp thing left me feeling a little jagged-edged. I don't think we're on the same wavelength, Wray Benson and I. Can't you think of another way to get this home?"

"Yeah. On the back of an apology. Now go down

there and try to be sweet. Maybe he felt under-appreciated as a rescuer, so approach from that angle. And tell him I'm the one that needs help. Shift it off of your shoulders onto mine so you won't be beholden to him afterwards… unless you want to be, of course."

"Oh, please." Circumstances began to overwhelm her reasoning. She cut one last look at the ugly footrest that forced the rectification and headed down the drive. "Time to put my big girl pants on and face the situation," she mumbled as she shouldered past another shopper. On her way, she tried not to think about how strong Wray Benson's arms seemed the day he fished her out of the trough. Only the water was cold. All the rest proved June-hot and bothered. She found him sitting on the weight bench while his friend talked it up with a prospective buyer down by the curb. Eyes closed and chin propped in his palm, he looked as though he might be praying.

"Excuse me, Wray." She stooped to make eye contact. He looked up and tried to blink away the troubled look she had glimpsed. She braced a knee on the pavement and attempted to steady herself for what came next. In need of a breath, she couldn't trust herself with the delay tactic. "About the lamps." Her throat choked closed with cotton, and she cleared it. "Wait. Please let me back up. Today, I'm not Lacey Woodhouse, the banker. I'm just a girl out with a friend shopping for discarded treasures who managed to toss the most splendid heroic gesture underfoot in the heat of the hunt." When she smiled a bit, he looked stunned.

"What I mean to say is, I'm amazed at your rescue of Julie and the lamps, your diving grab, and that diversionary boot-kick to softer territory. I let my greed for the glass mar my appreciation of your effort, and I somehow stung you with that shortcoming, but didn't intend to in the least. Could you accept my heartfelt apology for the fiasco earlier? I need to make amends." She dropped her second knee and crouched on her ankles, in hopes of a positive outcome. Seconds ticked by and it dawned on her that everything she'd just said would all seem phony once she sprang their need for transport help in its wake.

"I don't..." Wray shook his head.

She raised a palm to stop him. "Let me say this. Julie needs your help down the block but I'm not down here trying to butter you up on her account. The Holy Spirit convicts the believer of guilt and I've got a burning case of indigestion right now. Could we please settle this?"

"Well, I'll be." He sat up straight as though he half believed her. "You *can be* as enjoyable to be around as you are to look at, after all. What I tried to say is that I didn't exactly come across as the compassionate Christian back there either. If you'll forgive me for my harsh 'break apart' words, then I'll forgive you and we can draw the peace accord to get on with Julie's next request." He smiled and reached out a hand to seal the pact.

"Okay...I mean, better than okay. Thank you, Wray." She placed her hand in his. After the handshake, he pulled her up as he stood and she somehow tumbled forward. He rectified that in short order. This time no cooling trough water came splashing in to dampen his effect on her as she stood off-balance in his grip, way too close for comfort. "Guess you'd better hold off on the hug until we both really mean it." His gaze danced with mischief.

She dusted his shirt pocket with her fingertips and managed to step away to a safer distance, one from which her head seemed to clear enough to work. She tried to cinch down the smile erupting on her face but didn't catch it in time.

He looked down the block. "About Julie, I guess she needs me again. Is the Saint Bernard back or what?" He started to cross the yard.

"Something bigger." She fell into step beside him. "She bought an ottoman that won't fit in her trunk."

He gestured toward the curb. "Sounds like she might need my truck."

"She wants to buy you lunch if you could help transport it to her place. I hope it's not too much to ask. You've got something going on here at the city-wide sale, I know." Her stomach fluttered as her nervousness turned to something less familiar that amped up every time he glanced her way.

"Lunch? Oh, twist my arm and make me go. I'll tell Gary and then bring the truck down." He paused and pointed to his vehicle. "Want a ride over?"

"No, I'll jog back down and give Julie the news. We're on the left past that big tree."

"And you're good with this—I mean me man-crashing into your girl party and all?"

"Better than good." She crossed her heart to make it authentic. When he laughed and backtracked toward his truck, she tried to fight through the squeeze that clamped her chest. What in the world caused that? Forgiveness didn't usually end in a buzz, but this time it sure had.

~

Wray wiped his mouth and lifted his forearm off the fancy glass table they were seated around. Some secret sauce had made the sandwich more than palatable, but he couldn't help being distracted. Across from him, Lacey rested a potato chip on her bottom lip and he watched its journey with interest. When she caught him staring, she appeased his guilt with a faint smile.

"Gerald says I have too much stuff." Julie swished what remained of her salad around the plastic container. "Someday, I'll have a bigger place and it won't seem all that crowded together." She paused to take a bite.

Wray laid his napkin down. "Bigger houses just beg for more stuff." He wrapped his sandwich paper around the napkin and looked for a place to dispose of it. Julie motioned over the counter with her fork, but Lacey slid off her stool the same time he did and insisted on making the deposit for him. In seconds, he saw the wisdom of it when she came back with a cookie platter in hand.

"Julie has a sweet tooth," she explained, making matching dimples appear on her cheeks.

"Another invisible vice—along with being a shopaholic." He took a double helping. A cell phone sounded on top of the bar and Julie twisted back to look at it.

"Oh, it's Gerald. I'd better take this. Wray, thanks for everything, the ottoman hauling and the rearranging that fell along with it. You've been a real sport." She swooped up the phone and headed for the back. That left him with her attractive garage sale partner.

"About your 'bigger houses' comment, I wanted to say how likeable your place is, so tranquil and quaint out in the country. To borrow a line from Goldilocks, I think it's just right."

"It's livable, I guess. Now my sister's house in Yoder—that's tiny to a fault. With two kids underfoot, she's got to make the most of every inch."

She leaned over the table. "I see a lot of run-down and ramshackle in my work, but your place retains its charm."

He popped the second cookie in his mouth and wondered what he should say, given her visit had started his doomsday clock. Maybe wisdom would strike him as the chocolate chips melted in his mouth.

"Anyway, a person's home only says so much about him or her. I'd hate to be judged by my apartment, as it lacks any redeeming prospect whatsoever. They transferred me to the main office last fall and it seemed adequate at the time. Guess I went two-for-two when I got the little red sports car."

"You wouldn't be the first city-slicker to fall for a touch of country charm." He stood, ready to take his leave. A look of mild shock flitted across her face and he couldn't separate out whether word or action had caused it. He took his hat off the back of the sofa and gave the room a final glance. "You know, this place would make one highfalutin yard sale."

"Don't even think about it." Her tone teased as she met him at the door. "I'll walk you down to the truck— something my mother taught me." She pulled the door open.

He waited for her to go out first, which equated to good manners and lent him the better view. The walk down ended in a stroll toward his tailgate and it struck him that this might be it. Since the farm would be redeemed in plenty of time, he wouldn't have the occasion to see Lacey again. He let that sit on the edge a few seconds, unsure what to do about it. To buy time, he slammed the tailgate shut.

"You know, there's a funny thing about kind favors." She flung a glance at her car across the truck's grill. "They seem to attract a payback. So if you ever need a small act of kindness, say from a city-slicker friend like myself, please don't hesitate to ask." She walked beside his truck and stood behind the door where she rested her chin on the bracket of his side-view mirror.

He took the occasion to let his gaze settle into the green pools that looked up at him, stirred by sincerity and the what-if of the moment. "Lots of noise in the city," he replied as he lifted her chin with a protective finger. He opened the door and slid into the driver's seat which broke his contact with her a moment sooner than he'd intended. "I mean, with noise like that, a man might not be able to hear a call for help from out yonder." He tried not to slam the door, but it seemed deafening.

"Then you might have to find another way to get my attention." She gave him a look that set the challenge against indefinite time as she stepped back onto the curb.

"You take care now." With a tip of his hat, he fired the engine and let the truck pull him away from her magnetic green eyes. About as unfinished as he'd ever left something, he savored the interplay over and over in his mind while the truck rolled out of the condo complex headed back to quaint countryside.

Chapter 3

The bank's property division seemed unusually busy over the week, but for Lacey, the clock's arms had been tied in place. She picked up the file folder for a new foreclosure case and feigned interest because she already had a farm on her mind. From time to time, memories of a blue-eyed rancher with arms as strong as steel resurfaced. Somehow her daydreaming mechanism had been stuck on open throttle and she'd found it a little hard to focus on numbers. The familiar tinkle of a wrist full of charms caught her attention as a figure bent toward her.

Julie cocked an eyebrow. "We need to have lunch together—today." She tapped her pen on the corner of the desk. "I have something red-hot and want to run it by my romance advisor."

Lacey sat the folder aside. "Anything to put some space between me and this cubicle. I think I might be having a delayed case of spring fever or something."

"Honey, this heat doesn't say 'spring' to me," she

quipped. "I'm already running the air conditioning in the condo."

"Maybe I just want to be outside," Lacey added. A vision of a daisy-filled meadow popped into mind and she tried to blink it away. "Lunch sounds perfect. I don't know why we're so busy when the newspaper says the recession is over and things are turning around."

"Don't you understand how the paper works? It talks *at* the people instead of *for* the people. Maybe they could whitewash the contents back toward the truth instead of leaving it to yellow on the front porch of our decision-making capabilities."

"I hope lunch isn't going to be this deep," Lacey replied. "All I want is a chicken salad sandwich and to hear about someone else who really has a personal life."

"Oh, I've got enough sauce to make your chicken salad cluck." Julie pointed at the clock.

Watching her walk away in her neat, tailored suit left Lacey grateful to have an older confidante willing to discuss heart issues. Twenty-five minutes wasn't too long to wait, given she had been on slow burn all week.

~

His shoulders ached but at least the barn smelled better, Wray admitted as he forced the wheelbarrow around the garden to the compost pile. He stopped as the front bumper met the heap he had already accumulated and lifted the wooden arms to dump the load. As he walked the front wheel back, he shook the last of the hay straw out to end the morning's task. Since he'd been keeping the horse down in the river pasture and all the cattle had been sold, this cleanup job would last awhile—which brought some relief.

He rolled the empty wheelbarrow toward the water pump for its final washout, being somewhat aware that the goats shadowed him along the inside of the corral. The kid slipped out under the fence but a throaty warning from his nearby watchdog made it skitter right back in. He dropped the handles and picked up the priming bucket, an action that seemed to make the goat herd start whining.

"I know. She spoiled you all rotten." He swung the bucket through the air to shoo them away. As he walked by the elm toward the water trough, he glanced at the wooden bench, half expecting to see the red high heels that had occupied the spot last week. That talisman had occurred two dreams and countless daydreams ago, if he wanted to be honest. When he arrived at the water trough to dip his bucket, he didn't recognize his own reflection.

"So tell me why you can't stop thinking about her," he said to his water-image, which disappeared when the bucket submerged. "Yeah, you're definitely all shook up." He stepped back toward the pump. While one hand poured in the prime water, the other flexed the pump handle as the ancient mechanism remembered its function and wheezed until well water sloshed from the spout. He pumped as the bottom of the wheelbarrow became an ephemeral pond until he responded to the muscle ache on top of his right shoulder and quit. He sloshed the water around the sides of the wheelbarrow and decided to let it soak for a while.

From the sun's height, lunch should come next but he wasn't much in the mood. He traced the horizon beyond the elm with his gaze, stepped around the corral, and stopped to pull some untrimmed grass for the goats. He wandered past the barn and the next thing he knew, he was on his way down to the river pasture. A weathered wooden post jutted into the path about midway down and he tossed his sweat-soaked shirt onto it for safekeeping as he passed. His boots kicked up two meadowlarks on the way down, and they took to the opposite side of the fence where they perched together.

"She'd like it down here—if she'd ever come back," he admitted aloud, with no one but the gnarled hedge trees to hear his confession. The rest of the trip down to the water's edge became an aqueous daydream about what might have been if things could only be different.

~

Lacey picked at the curved sandwich on her plate that represented lunch.

"Gerald is taking me to Riverfest this Friday." Julie leaned over her colorful salad to emphasize her comment. The guys in the table next to theirs turned raucous when the waitress arrived with their oversized burgers.

Always on the loud side, Lacey disliked the microbrewery but Julie had a fondness for Old Town at lunchtime because that's where the happening people hung out. Despite Lacey's geometric print blouse and lime green pencil skirt, her wallflower act wanted to take the stage.

"Okay—what's with the long face? Something's up with you, and I'm not letting you excuse it away as spring fever," Julie insisted.

Lacey gave her a guilty look and put down her fork. "The lamp rescuer's been on my mind and I don't know what to do about it."

A sinfully satisfied look bubbled up on her lunch companion's face as the die-hard vegetarian attacked her harmless salad. The woman clawed her fork through the air in circular motion as though to prod for more information while her mouth became occupied with chewing.

"Let's start at the farm visit where I had to wait for the absent landowner. Hot as blazes, I sat by a water trough when his dog chased a baby goat back into the pen and knocked me in, kersplash."

Julie's eyes bulged and the fork carved up more air.

"Well, that's it really—except for the part where Wray hauled me out with arms like steel bands, held me to his chest and carried me under the shade of an enormous elm tree to dry out."

"Tell me you weren't delivering an NOD for the bank when you went out there," Julie replied.

Lacey picked up her water mug and wondered if she should fabricate something at this point. She took a drink and thought the better of it, ready to face the truth of what had transpired. "Technically, it was well past quitting time when the encounter took place, if that helps punch me off the clock."

Julie shook her head and picked up her water glass to give it further contemplation. "Did you make the presentation after that?" She sipped the water.

"Not only did I make the spiel, I did it nearly naked as my blouse literally turned invisible at the dunking." She brushed her fingertips down the front of her outfit.

Julie lost the sip of water, mostly through her nose, and scrambled to get her napkin to her face to mop up the surprise. Once she regained her composure, she kept the interrogation going. "So how did you feel at the second encounter—at the city-wide yard sale?"

"Ill at ease to the point of being rude during the battle for the lamps, which led to the need for my apology. Something happened between us after that. I don't know, Julie. He made some quip about me equally nice to look at and be with which led to my stumble over a handshake. Once again, I found myself in his grasp, like gravity intends to work against me now." She cut at the tip of the croissant and downed the chicken salad for caloric stability.

"Providence is working *for* you, my dear. And like gravity, you shouldn't resist it."

"I told him I'd be happy to repay the favor, a strong hint that he should call, but I don't know if country boy got the message. At this point, I have to leave it up to him."

"I don't think you have to translate for him just because he speaks country, Lacey."

Regret began to weigh against the casual conversation. She searched for a way to bring the personal topic to a close and remembered Wray's puzzling comment. "He wants to take me down to the river—whatever that means."

"Don't they all?" Julie winked and devoured a button mushroom in one genteel bite.

~

Starving by the time he made his way up from the river pasture, Wray ate everything in the refrigerator, which didn't equate to much. He'd have to grab some groceries on his next trip in town. Not that he was trying to think up reasons to go by the bank, but a man did have needs to address now and then. He popped the top on some canned peaches when the phone rang from the hall. He caught it by the second ring but had to hesitate while the peach slice found the down chute to his stomach. He wiped his mouth with the back of his free hand. "River Ranch."

"Uncle Wray-Wray, it's me."

"Hey there, Me. Is Josh there with you?" The tug on his heartstrings hit hard. A giggle followed as someone wrestled the phone away from the boy.

"Hi Wray, hope you're having a good week," a familiar voice said. The boy rattled on a mile a minute in the background and she tried to hush him to no avail.

"Hey Wren. Sounds like someone is worked up about something."

"Only because Mr. Jed gave him some hard candy the minute we walked into the meat store. I brought in some of my cinnamon apple rings to sell, but that's the final few jars from last year's crop. I hope the fruit trees in your yard are looking good."

"Things are looking up in every department."

"Well, that sounds more optimistic than usual. Do you have some news you can share with your darling sister?"

"I have some good news and some bad news—you pick."

"You know I always go for the good news first."

"Good news it is then. I think I may have found somebody—you know—smart, pretty and who doesn't seem to mind my most glaring flaws at first notice."

"That's great news, Wray, really great. Have you asked her out yet?"

"Not exactly. We just met last week."

"Ask her to come this weekend—to the fundraiser.

We'd love to meet her."

"That might be pushing it a little."

"You mean pushing you, right?"

"Okay—both. She owes me a favor, so maybe she'll come by."

"Listen big brother, no woman is going to just happen by the homeplace. Think of a creative way to leave her a note and see if she'll come to Yoder. We'll have entertainment aplenty, so it won't be hard to have a fun day together."

"Good point, except for my lack of creativity in figuring the note thing out. I'll try to come up with something, I promise."

"Then I'll expect to see her since I have confidence in your innate charm."

He half-moaned at his predicament but the possibility of having company for the day shined a ray of hope. That thought progressed toward the reason for the fundraiser, a bad-news subject he hesitated to broach. Since he knew she'd called from a borrowed phone, he went ahead and asked.

"How's my princess today?" His tone softened.

"She's still weak from the last round. We won't know for six more weeks whether the doctor thinks it's enough."

"Wren, the bank sent out the foreclosure notice. My time clock is three months." A pause weighed against the conversation as they shared the pain of the situation. "That's the bad news in a nutshell—which is where we'll keep it for today."

"Wray, will you do me a favor and not cut it too close?" she whispered into the phone. "That clinched our original agreement and I expect you to keep your end."

"So I will. Now about Saturday, you can expect me around eight o'clock—unless the goats give me trouble."

"Your goats? Trouble? Oh, I can't even imagine," she teased.

His heart ached, knowing the deep water she had been wading through by comparison. "Tell her I plan to rush right in to see her—first thing. Is there anything I can bring?"

"Just yourself—and your new friend. Good-bye, Wray. We'll see you Saturday."

He couldn't hold Wren on the line because she always called from the meat shop. The Mennonite village of Yoder lived old school, and no one had phones or electricity in their homes. He placed the receiver back on the base and lonesome silence poured in right away. He stepped back into the kitchen, clicked on the radio and listened to the top of the hour news while he made out a grocery list. That kind of rote writing slid out with no problem, whereas romantic notes tangled up his pencil something fierce. Emptiness sat on the kitchen counter right beside him. He wanted to do it, but the question remained *how*?

Chapter 4

Seated at her desk, Lacey made a schedule for the new foreclosure case. The only kind of math she could manage, everything else required a continuum of focused concentration and she had none. Julie had come by twice since lunch, animated with hand signals each time. Today Julie had been networking with the REO section next door, as Lacey's supervisor, Mr. Odom, ran the gauntlet between both sections. A round-faced sixty-year-old with a receding hairline, he seemed swollen with too much authority. She did her part to keep the peace. Conflict aversion became an art. As long as she got her work done on time, he never had any complaints.

Julie passed by with a handful of papers and swished them to her back while she tugged at her ring finger. Lacey wondered why she even looked up to catch the suggestive signals unless it was better to be unfocused and amused than just airheaded and alone. Mr. Odom walked by with a tense expression. That man could hear the rustle of potential money from fifty paces.

Her back tightened, so she stood and walked to the front windows. Someone drove by the bank in a truck and she craned her neck to see the color of the paint. Only five thousand or so blue trucks made their homes in the Wichita area—and most stayed out in the country where they belonged. A summer intern at the far cubicle turned and gave her a sheepish grin. She walked back to her seat and glimpsed a YouTube video on his monitor. Perhaps her afternoon had been more productive than she thought. With only one more hour until quitting time, she could make it—as long as she didn't think about the weekend.

~

By four o'clock Wray had a grocery list in one hand and a personal note in the other, which he considered progress in the right direction. He should have gotten motivated earlier because now he faced rush hour traffic in town. Maybe that represented a noble way to spend time, given his current state of mind. Wray grabbed his hat and stepped out of the back door headed for the garage. The dog came up and brushed his leg.

"Stay and guard the fortress, Hank." He patted its neck as a reward. The dog swished its tail twice and trailed off beside the garage. Without further thought, he loaded into the truck and drove up the driveway on a dual mission when the lazy daisies in the adjoining pasture caught his attention. He hadn't picked any wildflowers since he was a kid but the price seemed right. Maybe she'd recognize them from her drive in the other day. He stopped the truck, got out, and slapped his pocket for the knife. Once he'd straddled the fence strands, he entered the pasture and headed right to the greatest concentration. He cut stems until he had a handful of wistful white sentiment.

Making it back to the truck, he threw open the toolbox and looked for something to bind the stems into a bunch. Farm supplies abounded, and he found a nice length of twine under the fence pliers. He wound the line around until the flowers stayed in a tight bundle and knotted it securely, then tried to come back and retrofit a bow to it. With her answer hanging in the balance, this had better come together to do the trick, or he'd be by himself this weekend.

In the truck again, he turned onto River Road and headed for town at breakneck speed. The bank would close in an hour and the little red sports car would escape the parking corral like his kid goat. There would be no finding her after that, and he'd have to come home with a load of consolation groceries and some wilted wildflowers. Once he hit the pavement, he could make up some lost time. A rooster tail of dust soon obliterated everything in his rearview mirror.

~

Done for the day, Lacey and Julie walked to the bank's rear exit together.

Julie bumped her shoulder. "Tell me if he calls."

Lacey flashed a grimace for a good-bye and stepped toward the back of the lot, shielding her eyes from the simmering sun. She fished for the keys in the bottom of her purse and hit the unlock button as she gazed around the downtown setting. Was this truly where she wanted to be, in brick-and-mortar land? With the car door open to vent the June heat, she tried to think about her weekend. A hot breeze bounced off the corner building and something moved on the front of her windshield.

Her jaw fell open as she leaned forward and spotted a bouquet of daisy flowers all tied up with twine. Beautiful and wild, they didn't belong in a bank parking lot, but they'd somehow found her car. Lifting them with delicate admiration, she disappeared inside the car and turned on the ignition to get the air conditioning started. Time stood still as she cradled them in her lap, her hair blowing in her face from the dashboard fan. As she turned the bundle to admire it from every angle, a white cylinder of paper appeared under the tied bow. Her stomach knotted— the floral sentiment seemed to hold another message, one with words meant for her. She would take it out and have a look, but not here.

Rush hour traffic gnarled up ahead and she decided to exit off Douglas and head for the river. Once she passed the rounded façade of Century II, she turned the car south and thought of the water wall weeping in front of a high-end hotel. In less than a minute, she sat in a parking slot overlooking the Arkansas River as it flowed by the thriving municipality of four hundred thousand residents, none of whom seemed to notice either her or the delicate river.

With only the bouquet and her keys, Lacey stepped out onto the grassy hill and approached the riverfront as it lowered to a pedestrian walkway. About halfway down, she chose a private spot and sat. She glanced at the river and a flock of shorebirds along its bank. Her forehead pressed to her knees, she slowed her breathing and whispered a prayer for grace. Eyes open and expectant, she pulled the tucked note out of hiding and read its contents.

Join me for a fundraiser in Yoder this Saturday. Come out Friday evening for prep and stay in our stellar guest facilities. Old-fashioned fun—no high heels...Thinking of you, River Rancher

She fell back on the grassy hill and covered her eyes with one hand while the other clutched the flowers against her chest. The words twirled through her consciousness as excitement and apprehension battled it out in her heart. A murmur from the river inched up the bank toward her as though imparting some secret affirmation. A tear filtered some of the background confusion away as carefree clouds coasted uninhibited overhead. After countless minutes, she knew what she had to do. Now if only she could allow herself the freedom to do it.

~

A phone call would have been nice, Wray admitted. Two days spent setting things neat around the house and barn wasn't his normal focus, even though he could see a speck of value in it. No need to live like a hog just because you're by yourself, after all. Busy hands seemed to keep his mind off of her. He walked into the kitchen to give it a final inspection when the dog alarm went off out front. As he turned to exit out the front door, he picked up his hat from the stool and quit his maid job for higher pursuits.

One glance at the front yard gave him indigestion right about belt level. The neighboring rancher from down the road had one leg out of his fancy new truck and stood frozen under the dog's warning. He let it go on a second or two longer than was truly neighborly, just because it wasn't every day one got the upper hand.

"Away, Hank." He pointed back toward the barnyard. The dog dropped its ears but gave a final growl in its retreat from the stand-down. Instead of addressing the intruder as welcome company, he tipped his hat and stepped forward to see what the man wanted. They had never been close, even when his father was alive, which he semi-regretted since neighbors in these parts came miles between.

"Afternoon, Wray," the older man said. "I was just coming back from my Friday errands and thought to stop by and check in on you."

"Mighty considerate of you, Darold. I'm doing fine. Hope you're enjoying this heat wave set to kick off June."

"No, a man my age doesn't appreciate early heat. Better to get used to it over the slow course, but this is Kansas, so we expect the unexpected. Say, I didn't see your cattle as I drove out this morning. Have they gotten out?"

Wray saw where this was going and planned to head it off. "Not because they want to be. That pasture fence is strong enough to last forty years."

"Oh. All right then, I'll keep a watch from my side of things this summer. I know you're alone down here. We wouldn't want the Last Mohican at River Ranch to up and wash down the Arkansas River, now would we?"

"I'm not going anywhere, Darold. Give Mrs. Henley my best, will you? Tell her she can come pick apples this fall if the Good Lord keeps them watered."

"I'll do that, Wray. You take care now. See you around." The man's greedy gaze wandered around the farmhouse grounds before he slid back into his toy truck.

A sick feeling passed through Wray's gut. With a squint, he pulled his hat lower and decided to make a perimeter check to be sure things were ready for welcome company—if he'd find favor enough to have some. He'd know sometime in the next two hours but until then, he'd have to settle for a nosy neighbor and an elm tree full of cawing blackbirds. The goats bleated once he rounded the garage and he threw up his hands in absolution. "She's coming back today—and everything will be right in your little worlds again."

~

This had to rank right up there with the craziest things she had ever done. Lacey shifted her gaze into the floorboard where a wicker picnic basket cradled the dinner she had packed for them. Maybe Wray would carry it down to this river spot he'd mentioned, or maybe the porch swing would turn friendly. The whole deal seemed fraught with unknowns, but the thought of staying at her apartment wondering what could have been didn't hold half a candle to coming out and living it. This washboard road had shaken up the bottle she'd been living inside. The bridge came into view and she slowed to enjoy the way the land surrendered to its influence. More wildflowers danced in the late afternoon breeze and swept their ease over her.

Prayer stitched its way into her feelings as the flood control berm popped up on the far edge of the farm field she drove beside. She prayed for God to unfold his blessing on her as she stepped out in faith to find her place. This particular landscape held appreciative beauty, and she expressed that to the

Creator of all rivers and the watersheds stretching in between them. As the gate came into view, she ended the prayer and glanced in her rearview mirror for one last self-inspection. She had dressed down in comfortable clothes, a tank top under her V-neck tee shirt in case things got wet again—or too hot.

Beneath the arched entrance, she rolled the windows down and studied the daisy patch. In nature's random fairness, she couldn't pick out a thin portion anywhere in the meadow. How generous of God to put so many wildflowers out here where almost no one could enjoy them. Maybe that reflected his lavish character. She hoped he had spared some blessings for her—beyond the bouquet she had already received but in similar fashion. As she passed the lilac bush, she nosed the car in front of the house until the resident rancher appeared in the side yard. With a smile, he beckoned her toward the garage. Okay. She had arrived. God help her now.

~

"Thank you, Lord." Wray stepped around the back of Lacey's sports car to help her get out. When her bare legs appeared first, his pulse shot a rapid-fire echo across his eardrums. He offered her a hand, which she accepted with a little smile. Shed of her tense banker demeanor, she seemed relaxed, almost radiant. "Welcome back to River Ranch."

She took her sunglasses off and poked them into her hair as they stood in the shade cast by the garage. "Maybe I'm a girl with a weak spot for daisies." She smiled as her gaze searched his face.

He couldn't get much past her green eyes, as today they seemed like pleasurable pools that didn't spark like flint. Wray allowed himself to stand there an extra instant so he could relish their closeness. She didn't seem in any hurry, and he didn't want to rush right back into chores. "As bouquet invitations go, it might not get any better than this." He motioned toward the barnyard and its rim of trees.

She flashed a quick grin as though she had a secret. "Well, in that case, I hope this picnic basket doesn't go to waste." She nodded toward the floorboard. "Any chance I can get some help to unload?"

His eyebrows cocked as he followed her gaze, saw the big basket, and pounded his fist on his chest. "Tell me what you need. We can put your things inside the back porch for now so they're not out here in the heat."

"That's great. I wouldn't want my candles to melt."

He gave her a puzzled look as she approached her trunk and then shook his head with a snicker. "You can't have candles where you're headed." He lifted her overnight bag and slammed the trunk lid.

Her eyes widened in surprise. "Why not? Where's this stellar guest quarters you mentioned in the note?"

He headed toward the passenger door to snag the picnic basket. "That's stellar as in star-filled." With the basket locked in his grasp, he closed the door with his hip and nodded toward the barn. "I've got you set up in the hayloft—I think you'll find it more than comfortable." When her expression animated, that said it all. He had intended to impress her with his one-of-a-kind accommodations and he'd accomplished it.

"I've always admired the shabby-chic look." She followed him toward the back porch as her purse dangled from her shoulder.

"If that's girl-talk for having straw in your hair, I

think you're gonna be in heaven." He opened the back screen door and led her into something of a sunroom his grandfather had added to the back of the house. He placed her bag on a loose-cushioned sofa and walked the picnic basket into the kitchen.

"Wray, this is so quaint, it's adorable." She scanned the perimeter of the kitchen, which halted at the light-filled window over the sink. "I hope you haven't gone to a lot of trouble on my account." She opened the basket, pulled plastic tubs out and stuck them in the refrigerator.

He fingered some water drops on the rim of the sink. "Nope. Don't consider it trouble." Whatever the opposite of trouble could be, that's what his veins flushed with at the moment. He needed a breeze, and he needed it quick.

Chapter 5

I didn't see Hank when I came in." Lacey started to close the picnic basket.

Wray leaned against the sink with his arms folded against his chest. "He's on kid-goat duty out behind the corral."

She pulled a bag of baby carrots out next and waggled them at him. "I brought some goat candy— hope you don't mind."

"They seem willing to eat anything, so go ahead and try. You've already spoiled them with the plucked grass. Now they follow me every time I pass by the pen."

"You'd think they would figure out who to count on, if they have any smarts at all."

"Oh, you'd be amazed how diabolical and premeditated those critters can be, so don't say I didn't warn you." He gave a laugh.

She shut the basket lid and dropped the carrots on the table. "What's on the agenda first? Shouldn't I see the rest of the fairytale cottage?"

"Okay Snow White, come right this way and we'll circle the floor plan for your entertainment. Don't blink!"

"Hey, I like small floor plans because it forces you to use your space wisely."

"That might actually work if your space wasn't also a generational museum. That's what happens when you live at the homeplace—stuff tends to accumulate." They stepped into a dining room anchored by a glass-fronted oak buffet.

She stopped to examine it and enjoyed a row of little glass birds of various sizes. Dust coated everything inside the cabinet, which hinted of neglect. "Was this your grandmother's piece?" She hoped to start a dialogue to find out a little more about him.

He nodded and stuffed his hands in his pockets. "This is how I was taught to walk through this room as a boy. Now I use the far end of the table for an office at tax time, so I can leave the paperwork out for easy reference."

"How about I promise to dust out this cabinet for you some rainy day? Glass is my soft spot. I'd love to touch those delicate little birds in there. That's part of the joy of my stained glass hobby, getting to handle the delicate glass."

"My sister quilts which sounds about the same, fitting little pieces into big picture format." He fashioned a square with his fingers.

She turned to him, delighted with the last revelation, and wanted to probe a little more. "You mentioned your sister and her children before. I hope I get to meet her."

His eyes twinkled at her interest. "Try tomorrow, unless we don't get our work done this evening. Then I might be afraid to show my face." Wray disappeared through the next doorway.

"She lives in Yoder?" She followed him into the adjoining room. A brown plaid sofa gave the room a strong masculine feel but she found places of redemption, like the beautiful bay window. She stepped in front of it and remembered her first visit there in the swing.

He stood in front of the screen door. "My mother's family lived in Yoder. My dad sort of stole her away to live out here."

She knew little about Yoder's Mennonite heritage. "Did they live the simple life?"

He shuffled his feet and straightened the doormat. "Yes, in Yoder, but Mom made the adjustment and enjoyed modernization once they moved here. My sister kind of stepped back into it by accident. She fell in love with a Yoder farmer and embraced his way of life."

She stopped in front of a collage of aged photos. "Come show me who everyone is."

In a second, he stood behind her and gazed over her shoulder. "That's my dad and grandpa with the Allis-Chalmers tractor up in the corner. Next to them, grandma stands with all of dad's siblings. Moving on a generation, that's me with my little sister, Wren. She followed me everywhere in those days."

"Sorry she gave up on you." Lacey tried to keep a straight face with the tease.

He leaned in close to her ear and drew in a breath. "Oh, to have those simple days back," He stepped through the hall doorway and led the way into the unknown.

Three doors opened off the central hall and the center one was ajar, revealing a tile floor. She assumed it was the bathroom. His tour seemed to be losing its audio so she prompted him. "And which one is your room?" She held up both arms, one in each direction. He clapped the right hand and she recalled the curtain moving off that corner of the house. "You were watching me in the orchard the other week, weren't you?"

"Well, since I don't have too many strangers come dance through my apple trees, I thought I'd better pay attention. You know, in case you were an angel or something."

The occasion of their initial encounter flashed to mind next but Lacey wouldn't allow it to stay. "I guess you use the other room for storage?" The door was shut tight.

"It holds Wren's baby stuff mostly, but there's some of Mom and Dad's things, too."

"Is Wren hoping to have more children?" As soon as she asked, a dark look clouded his expression. Maybe she'd just stepped on a land mine.

"She lost her husband four years ago, the same time we lost Mom and Dad," he replied, "in a grain elevator accident. The dust ignited, they determined after-the-fact. Most families in Yoder had at least one family member perish. Thank God Wren was safe at home with a toddler, my nephew Josh, and my niece, Pleasance, who was seven at the time."

She touched his arm and let their gaze connect so he could sense her sincerity.

"The Mennonite Relief Fund covered expenses for

most of the victims, but the money ran short. Since they considered Dad an outsider, the Benson family never received any of the disbursement, but Wren did get Josiah's burial paid for, thank goodness." He took a breath and looked at her, a hint of the jagged-edged truth on his features. "Dad already had plots paid for up at Maple Grove so I followed through for him."

"That's how you inherited River Ranch?" She bowed her head so she had to peer up through her lashes.

He fixed his gaze on her as deafening seconds passed. "Yes, plus the second mortgage Dad indebted himself with to update our equipment. In total irony, he didn't get to live long enough to work the loan off and both new grain trucks went out with him in the explosion."

Weighed by the gravity of Wray's story, a flash of an idea came to redeem part of the equipment loss, but she'd have to do more investigation before she'd be bold enough to pitch it to him. The tragedy burdened him enough without having to give him false hope of recovery and then it not pan out. She worked for a bank, after all, so she could manage a little scouting. "But you're still here—and so is the farm. That has to count for something."

He opened his mouth to speak and must have thought better of it. He cleared his throat instead.

She needed to turn the somber mood around. "So, could I sweet talk you into eating dinner before going out? Otherwise, the goats will have to share their carrots."

At the mention of food, Wray perked up. "That would be a real hardship for all involved. Sure, let's eat first then and I'll make you work it off later this evening."

She smiled as she doubled back toward the kitchen to assemble the food she'd taken from the picnic basket. She soon found herself humming.

~

Wray stretched at the table. "We probably have less than three hours of daylight left to get our prep work done. I'm in charge of livestock sales for the fundraiser tomorrow."

Lacey glanced up from the sink with a puzzled look. "Translate prep work for me." She reached for the bag of carrots.

He'd have to gloss their next task up a bit, since fencing didn't register as glamorous as far as chores went. "You know how that kid goat is constantly getting out of the corral?"

"Yes, I'm familiar with his wandering folly."

"Well, we're making a portable playpen to sort of contain that waywardness so my livestock doesn't sneak around downtown Yoder behind my back."

"A playpen then?" Her lips seemed to toy with the words.

"Maybe even two. Let's see how it goes once we get cranking."

She stepped toward him and placed her free hand into his. "I'm here to help—that's why I came, but you may have to teach me how to be a good assistant." She tilted her face up and a luminous smile erupted.

Wray's chest tightened. Lord help him, how was he going to get anything constructive done in proximity to that? "I'll lead and you follow—how does that sound?"

"Um, I like it as long as it doesn't involve power

tools."

"Nope, no power tools. Just a stapler for you and some good old fashioned elbow grease." He allowed himself to enjoy the rich green lure of her eyes. "Besides, a stapler is fairly non-gender as far as hand tools go. Just pretend you're doing upholstery work."

She bounced the carrot bag in her hand. "Like a padded playpen? Now I'm getting a better picture. I'm ready, willing, and able, but could I feed the goats before I start?"

He released her hand and reached for his hat with a quick wink. "Spoil away. I'll start with laying out the fence posts. I don't suppose you brought a hat?"

"I most certainly did." She flounced down the sunroom steps and soon topped her jet-black hair with a prissy bright pink cowgirl hat.

Struck by the stark beauty of the color contrast, Wray tore through the back door while he still had the motivation. Work, it kept a man honest.

~

Happy that the carrot bag had been nibbled half-empty, Lacey snapped the staple gun shut and surged with energy. She placed the tool on the wooden bench under the elm and walked over to the barn where Wray had disappeared.

She swept the cavernous interior with her gaze. "Are you still in here?" When she recalled her earlier reaction to the barn's repugnant odor, she noted that it smelled only earthy today—maybe even sweet with hay.

Wray leaned over the rail from the upper floor. "Up here. I need to throw these spools down to you. Are you game?"

She pushed her pink cowgirl hat back on the crown of her head. "Go ahead, I'm a pretty good catcher."

He faked a toss to test her reaction time and then let the spool go. As it tumbled down, it took the form of a comet, leaving a plastic tail attached to his hands as the spool traveled downward. A few feet short of her grasp, the strapping ran out.

She grabbed the empty spool from midair. "Wray? What just happened?"

His snickers rained down on her from the loft rail above.

She tried not to feed his tomfoolery with a smile. "Okay, Mister Trickster, I guess at some point you'll give me the whole thing."

He pled innocent with a shrug of his shoulders, which seemed to cause the release of the upper strand, as it fell down about her like a pot of spaghetti noodles. This time his laughter fell like a waterfall.

Not willing to play into his hands, she wound the surplus of strapping with business-like efficiency and centered it around the spool.

"I have four more rolls," he warned between snickers. "That was just a test."

She walked a few steps closer, planted her hands on her hips and looked up at him. "Let's proceed under the assumption that we are not having any trust issues between us."

Wray had already picked up the second spool. He now hesitated at the rail and rested the fencing supply on his shoulder. Atlas-like up there, the barn's roof beams stretched above him. "I'll tell you what. If you can catch four more of these spools, I'll give you a preview of your sleeping quarters."

She clapped without hesitation "That's totally a deal, River Rancher." Maybe she should disclose her tenure as the third baseman of her high school softball team, but he really hadn't given her much lead-in time. A spool came cascading downward and she caught it in the double crook of her arms. She escorted it toward the door and stepped back into firing range, where the next launch waited. When he arched this spool out with an underhand toss, she had to backpedal but made a clean catch nonetheless. She rolled it toward the doorway and did a little shuffle step to match his new position down the rail.

She blinked and saw two spools heading toward her, one right after the other. The first one she snagged double-handed, slid it off her left hip and got ready to catch the last one in her right hand. He gave a renegade yell to distract her, but the last fly ball headed toward her destined for an out. She cradled the spool along her right arm, trapping it against her ribs.

Wray applauded in amicable defeat.

She stood askant, more than ready to see her guest suite. "So where's the elevator up?" When he indicated a wall along the barn's narrow end, she ran for it, delighted to join him. Racing up the built-in ladder, she soon stood in ankle-deep hay.

He moved toward a set of double doors, slid the brace board free, and opened the hayloft to the great outdoors. Sunlight drenched the golden hay. Reminiscent of a little clubhouse, the nook was bounded by a set of shelves dotted with nature treasures on one side and a hammock hanging across the other. A white slatted chair held a heart-shaped pillow trimmed in lace with a button in the center.

"This was Wren's hideout when she needed some space," he confessed. "She liked to collect little things from the outdoors."

"Like fresh lilacs?" She stepped over to touch the blossoms stuffed into an aqua-tinted canning jar. She held the jar up toward the doors and sunlight filtered through the water like a magic prism.

"Most people would sniff them first," he teased, dimples showing on both cheeks now.

"For me, it's all about the color." She returned the flowers to the shelf.

"I brought some old quilts from the house earlier and folded a pillow or two inside, so you can make your bed as fluffy as you'd like."

"This is definitely shabby-chic, except for being a little more authentic than most."

He extended his arms to frame the charm-packed space. "So, do you like it?"

She tiptoed into his span and gave him a quick shoulder hug for all his thoughtful efforts. Before he could reciprocate, she raced back to the top of the ladder in rapid escape. The goats needed entrapment, but she didn't. She needed to run wild and free. And right now, that meant a hasty climb down to earth. *Feet don't fail me now.* The worn wood of the ladder rungs came as reassurance she would command the getaway. When she made landfall, the Border collie gave a loud bark. "Run, boy, run." She broke into a trot to escape the barn and the dog followed close at her heels.

Chapter 6

Wray hammered the u-nail in place on the last fence post. He planted both knees to watch his assistant operate, two posts back. Lacey had proven fairly adept with the stapler as she forced the face of it against each post with a bulge of bicep and the grit of determination. They worked by moonlight now, as twilight faded to evening out in the barnyard. "That's it. Let's consider ourselves done. We're out of strapping anyway. Great job keeping up and manhandling that stapler, Lacey."

"I'm feeling it in my shoulders right about now."

He heard a tinge of satisfaction in her tone as he stood to collect his tools. The nail bucket sat half a length beyond her and he stretched his calves as he closed the gap. Unable to resist her squat position centered on the post, he allowed the side of his hammer to give her a friendly tap as he passed. She made a high-pitched karate noise and the stapler went off, finishing the post.

She rose to advance to the next post. "Hey, thanks for the added momentum."

He shoved his hat back "Don't mention it—I'm here to help."

She chuckled and fastened the strapping down the length of the wooden post.

His hammer rang out as it found the bottom of the metal bucket. Nails jangled with its impact. Wray watched her with satisfaction. "I'm going to roll this first one up and load it."

"I'll be right behind you with this one." She fired off the stapler as though to prove it.

He knelt and let out a late-in-the-day moan, which earned him another chuckle from the vicinity of the second fence.

The stapler sounded in staccato. Lacey stood and began to roll up her section of fence.

He tucked the last post through the lattice of the strapping. "You're a pretty good worker for a city girl." He lifted the fence roll and moved off to load it in the truck. A backtracking move, he met her where she labored with the second roll. To keep it from entangling, he tucked in the last post and took it out of her hands.

She walked along beside him and their shoulders touched. "So I'm pretty and a good worker, is that what I heard?"

He tossed the roll into the truck bed where it fell against the first roll and he pulled up the tailgate with a metallic slam. "Can I plead the Fifth, at least until I can get cleaned up and defend myself?"

"Well what about me? I bet my guest suite doesn't have any running water."

"No, ma'am. You'll have to come inside for that sort of creature comfort. Your digs are rustic and, what did you call it? Authentic, that's right. It's authentic hayloft." He received a slap on his shoulder and tucked his hands in his back pocket to keep from retaliating.

She glanced up over the orchard. "The sky's lovely out here."

He stopped and tried to see what she saw, but her profile kept distracting him. "Lovely all right. We'll be back out in stellar appreciation to settle you in later. How about you retrieve your bag and take a turn in the bathroom first? Sunrise comes earlier than you think and we have a big day tomorrow."

"You can tell me more about that up in the hayloft."

He opened the door and let her enter first like a true country gentleman, only to have Hank rush in behind her and cut him off. "Well, I can't tell you too many details, for fear that you might run away."

She slipped her hand onto the overnight bag's handle. "And forfeit my shabby-chic encounter? No way!" When his hand overlaid hers for possession of the bag, she succumbed to his good-natured chivalry. "I'm having a good time, Wray. Thanks for having me out. It's like a different world out here."

"It's not for everybody, just daisy-lovers and such." He caught a glimpse of the half-sized pie on the kitchen table as he passed by. "I hope that miniature pie didn't come just to weigh the picnic basket down."

"Maybe we can put it out of its misery after your shower. I'm first." She pulled her bag away from him with a grin and disappeared toward the hall. "Hope I can trust the two of you alone."

He bent to grab the dog's empty water bowl. "She hopes she can trust the two of us alone with an innocent pie. Hank, you're on barn duty tonight, so you'd better go get forty winks before your shift starts." The dog barked and wagged its tail until the dish found its way back to the floor. Wray turned on the hot water and lowered his forearms under the kitchen faucet. In seconds, the water pressure waffled and his thoughts turned to Lacey. Natural and unfettered by circumstance, their casual acquaintance seemed to hold the promise of something more. He lathered with a bar of soap and let the silkiness of it drain the roughness of the barnyard away.

~

Lacey propped her cosmetic case on the back of the toilet tank and examined the room as she shirked off her sweaty clothes. Rustic, the room featured barn-wood shelving stacked with mismatched washcloths and little bars of soap. An apothecary jar full of cotton balls looked untouched for decades, coated with an uninterrupted accumulation of dust. At least the tile surfaces appeared well scrubbed and the tub bore no dirt ring from its last occupant. She pulled her hair into a looped ponytail and clipped her bangs back.

With a twist of her wrist, the water flow burst forth, not a dainty drizzle from a conservation showerhead, but a dirt-busting pulse. In the country now, she liked everything about it. The water slapped her thigh as she stepped in and she heard Wray's footsteps in the hall, headed for his room. When she snatched the shower curtain closed, the hot water claimed her fully. She paused to let it massage her sore shoulders.

"Hey, save me some hot water," he called through the bathroom door.

"You'll get your share." Unready to relinquish her present state of luxury, she reached for her moisturizing face soap. "At least I hope you'll get your share," she whispered to the shower walls as she dipped her shoulders under the forceful flow.

~

Wray waited on the loft ladder as Lacey made the climb with a flashlight in her hand. He brought a battery-powered lantern that would lend her sleeping quarters a soft glow until she was ready for lights out. His position gave him the perfect vantage point for inspecting the back of her calves, which appeared smooth and lightly muscled as they tapered into thin ankles. Maybe he should do less looking and more conversing to help fight the physical magnetism drawing him toward her.

"Almost there. You can't be too careful, as everything looks different at night." He attempted to hold the lantern higher for her benefit. She gained altitude faster with the improvement, when the dog started to whine down below. "Don't worry, Hank old boy. I'll be down in a few minutes." The ascending ankles seemed to slow again and he wondered if it was something he said.

"You'll stay long enough for me to get comfortable, won't you Wray?" She halted her footwork as she waited for his reply.

"Oh sure. I can handle the chic cove for short bursts, anyway. I'm not much of a night owl though. If I stop answering your questions, that means I've fallen asleep."

"I'll try to be more interesting than that," she promised, and stepped up several rungs.

His climbing mechanics shifted to automatic as he evaluated what "more interesting" might entail. If magnetism ever led to combustion, then being situated in a hayloft with an attractive woman seemed counterintuitive to a man who typically played it safe.

I'm not sure I can handle more interesting this late in the day. When her feet disappeared above the ledge, he surfaced to find her squared around, waiting for him.

Her eyes twinkled in the lantern light and her skin seemed to glow. "Just being together is enough, country boy." Her words trailed off in a lopsided grin. The accompanying dimple dent made him misplace his handhold, so she claimed the lantern and left the flashlight in the hay.

A glow infiltrated the chic nook. He pulled himself over the ledge and retrieved the silver cylinder to conserve its light beam. He threw the brace beam and opened the hayloft doors to get some cross ventilation. "We'll draw more mosquitoes with the light on," he informed her. "And it will spoil one of my last surprises for you tonight."

Lacey's face animated as she stepped back to click the lantern off. She situated a small drawstring bag and joined him at the loft's edge.

When her shoulder nudged against him in the pitch dark, he felt sparks even if he didn't see them. "Help me spread this quilt out so we can take a long look."

"Wray, I can't see a thing. Where's the edge?"

He could hear an ounce of fear in her voice and pulled her to his right side. "Get these back corners."

His eyes acclimated to the dark. He crossed the door opening and straightened the far corner, then returned to the quilt's center. "Now drop down on your stomach and look out into the night sky." He knelt and soon felt the quilt compress into the hay beside him as she worked into position near the edge. With the moon rising late, he knew the first part of the night would be a star-studded spectacular.

Lacey shifted closer to the door opening but didn't say a word.

Into the mix of silence and darkness came a scent that made him think of something baking in the kitchen. Under the pretense of smoothing the lumpy hay under the blanket, he shifted toward her until their shoulders touched. He heard her draw a deep breath and decided to let her take in the star show uninterrupted. His gaze fell on the outline of the Big Dipper and he traced the handle back toward the farm. God's immenseness came to mind.

Lacey made several throaty acknowledgments and crept even closer to the edge.

He could make out her faint profile against the inky black. Her chin was propped in her hands. Maybe if he looked closer, he could see the stars in her eyes, so he leaned in to search.

"This is unspeakably magnificent," she said, staring out at the star-spattered night.

"I agree," he whispered, way too close for his own good. Maybe the huskiness in his voice made her turn toward him. He might have even felt the angel-wing brush of her hair on his shoulder. Then, there they were—the stars in her eyes. Suddenly his heart pounded a mile a minute and he couldn't feel his extremities.

"We'd better start chatting it up or I'm going to bolt over the edge here out of self-preservation."

She leaned away, arched her neck back, and laughed at him.

"Can I help it if you smell so delicious, like a muffin, and have somehow managed to catch a few stray stars in your eyes?"

"A muffin, huh? Maybe you're suffering from malnutrition instead of fatigue. My lotion has ginger in it."

"Tomorrow there should be food galore. Wren's fixing a chicken noodle dinner for her part of the fundraiser and the Yoder bakery has promised dessert. Maybe by midmorning you could mosey over there and lend her a hand."

"That sounds better than tending livestock, but I don't want to abandon you."

"It's their Heritage Days festival this weekend, which means there will be a good crowd in town. The tractor pull runs on-and-off all morning, so Wren plans to be set up and ready when that lets out. My livestock-selling business will come and go, so we've decided to use the silent auction approach of taking bids throughout the day."

"Ha! That can get more than a little interesting as the last few minutes wind down, based on my experience. The bank holds a charity art auction in the fall for the Children's Home. My friend Julie served as coordinator last year, so I became her ready assistant."

"Great, because I'm putting you in charge of the bid sheets." His elbow tingled from lack of circulation so he lowered onto his back and twisted his shoulder blades into the hay to get comfortable. She placed her hand on the crown of his left shoulder and left it there. A soothing wave of calm swept over his body.

"Help me learn who everyone is by calling them by name when they walk up, will you Wray?"

Before he could reply, something rustled faintly from the eaves. He reached for the flashlight in slow motion and tapped her hip with his other hand.

"Roll onto your back," he whispered. "We may have company." He felt her flip and move closer as she tucked up under his raised shoulder. The sound repeated itself and he aimed the cylinder at its source and clicked the beam on. Half a rafter's width over, the light revealed the culprits. Three wide-eyed owlets peered over their nest rim, huddled together. Lacey cooed in adoration and the sound eased over him like cotton. The loft turned cozy.

"Well, that explains some of the mess I found down below," he quipped. "I found owl pellets in the hay, likely where the mother perched on the nest hatching these guys."

"Turn the light off. You're scaring those puffballs to death." She reached across him. When he outmaneuvered her, she slapped at the flashlight like a playful cat. Giggles hatched at each unsuccessful foray. Now propped on her elbow in defeat, Lacey hovered over him.

The maniacal ginger muffin aroma seized his senses and his throat went dry.

Her mood seemed to turn more serious. "I'll have a sentinel above and below watching over me tonight. I like the thought of nature surrounding me while God oversees it all."

A curtain of her silky hair fell against his cheek

and a floral scent mixed with the kitchen aroma, triggering a visceral response under his ribs. Maybe he moaned or something, as she straightened and worked herself to her knees beside him. He switched the flashlight to his right hand and released it to the quilt.

"You must be tired Wray, so let's call it a night, as beautiful and filled with wonder as it has been."

He grunted a response, unable to land on a word that wouldn't betray him.

"I hoped we could pray together before you go—to release the day back to God—and maybe thank him for our friendship. How do you feel about that?"

Her words dipped a blessing on him like dew falling in the early dawn as her comfort seeped through him soul-deep, making it impossible to move. How odd to have someone beside him in the pitch black, someone who wanted to invoke a prayer over him. Maybe the nighttime held redemption from his lonely routine where daylight only seemed to shine on continual struggle. And perhaps she brought God a little closer to his hopeless predicament, if that were somehow possible. "You first," he managed.

Her slender fingers sought his and interlaced. Their grip held firm. "Lord of all Creation, we've found a beautiful combination of your work here tonight and want to acknowledge your sovereignty over it and thank you ever so much for it. May we never take it for granted—not for a minute. Forgive us for the things we didn't get exactly right today, which might include some of my stapling job. Help us have a good day tomorrow and let us be tenderhearted to the members of this quaint community. Also let me be good help to Wray and Wren so this fundraiser can be a huge success."

He felt the squeeze on his fingers but needed a few seconds to allow an emotional mist to clear before he could make his contribution. Her fingertips slid up and down his forearm to lend encouragement in the moment. "Father God, my first prayer is for Wren, who needs your abiding presence more than most. Help get her past these difficult times and back into fullness of life. Next, I thank you for bringing Lacey out here to River Ranch despite the circumstance of her arrival, which reminds us that you are Lord of the river bottom as well as the mountain heights. I know you are the source of every good and perfect gift—and she's the best one to come my way in longer than I can remember." He cleared his throat and her fingers slid over his again. He claimed them in a tight lock. "Lastly Lord, I ask you to put it in everybody's heart to be generous tomorrow on behalf of the fundraiser, and work your perfect will in that whole situation, especially toward Pleasant's comfort. In the holy name of our Savior Jesus Christ."

"Don't say 'amen,'" she insisted in a whisper. "That way we live the continual prayer."

Caught off-guard, he pushed back against the black night and sat bolt upright in search of closure of some sort. "Well—we need something," he replied, somewhat confused.

Her fingertips arrived into his quandary. She traced the stubble along his jaw line with a phantom touch as the ginger incense turned magnetic. Inexplicably, her breath and hair relayed the vulnerability of her nearness.

No longer at a total loss, he corralled her against

his chest and kissed her right on her parted lips. To add mercy to the benediction, she kissed him back. An ethereal moment with an angel in his arms, he found tender closure and a whole lot more.

~

"Now you really must go," Lacey confessed, short of breath and maybe willpower. The ambiance of the nook doubled with him there, but she would have the stars—and her dreams—once he departed.

The lantern clicked on and flooded the nook with light. "You bet. Pick your light source and let me have the other."

She weighed her options and clutched the flashlight to her chest.

Wray grabbed the lantern and stood to descend from the loft. "Just maybe I have a new respect for shabby-chic." His tone teased as he started down the ladder.

"Go back to your cottage style, Wray, it suits you better." She locked her gaze on him until he disappeared into the lower realm of the barn. This is where she belonged—up with the bevy of stars playing mother to a trio of puffballs. She overheard Wray speak to the dog. The barn door latched below, leaving her alone in the stellar guest quarters.

Called back in admiration of the constellation vista, Lacey touched the right bay door and allowed her toes to dangle over thin air. She made out patches of stars that swirled into charted patterns, crystal clear from her vantage point tonight. The scene made her realize how much she missed by living in the city—precious things like daisies, owlets, and baby goats. Now she could add to the treasury list a good-looking rancher who cared deeply about his family.

Cozy with thoughts of Wray, she stood and pulled the double door closed. She shoved the brace beam into its fitting, separating herself from the rawness of night. She stepped back onto the quilt and dropped to her knees. Making a rough estimate, she shot the light beam up and checked the twig bowl filled with puffballs. The owlets blinked back. She took that as code for all-is-well, then grabbed her drawstring bag and hoisted a pillow from the hammock. Their stargazing spot seemed to hold more appeal than a swaying mattress, at least to start the night.

She pulled at the drawstring of her bag, located and slid a tube of lip balm across her lower lip, popping the cap back on in one fluid motion. She pushed the pillow to the hollow spot where Wray had been and worked the hay lumps into level compliance. With one last pass of the light beam around her chic nook, she pressed off the flashlight and laid her head on the pillow. She lacked enough neck support, so she raked the drawstring bag beneath it and found the improvement adequate. With her hands folded across her heart, sleep began to overtake her senses as thoughts of a soft-lipped rancher shushed more worrisome mind-whispers away.

Chapter 7

Wray crossed the barnyard in record time as dawn tugged at the edges of the river prairie. He'd slept like a baby last night and couldn't shake the feeling that the day held promise. He glanced up at the loft doors and remembered the cadence of Lacey's voice as she prayed over him in the dark, so genuine and heartfelt. A man could get used to that, especially a man whose land teetered on the line. Today's activities would put his guest through her paces, so he'd watch and see how well she met the challenge.

He decided to hook up the livestock trailer before she awakened. She would have to lend a hand to load the goats though, or he'd risk a late departure. As he rounded the back of the barn, it occurred to him that he may not have mentioned that the goats represented his donation to the fundraiser. He hoped that wouldn't cause a rift between them, as being on the same page held more appeal, especially considering how their prayer had ended last night.

The trailer lay in front of him now, its tongue pigeon-toed toward the barn. It might be shaky ground for a rancher to mull over kisses to a woman that smelled like a spice rack. He kicked the trailer tongue straight and stepped around to unlatch the loading door. If his thinking got this sidetracked while alone, what would it be like while they worked together all day? He grunted in response and retraced his steps back toward the garage. He hopped into his truck and backed out which left her sports car by its lonesome self. The scene messed with his head a little.

Wray braced his arm across the seat back and pressed the gas pedal, backing the entire way to the hook-up. Close enough, he set the brake and slid from the cab. Without its usual bad attitude, the tongue hovered over the ball while he cranked up the jack stand until the hitch caught. Now he needed the goats to line up and file in so he could be on his way. Fat chance.

With a determined jerk, he pulled the rig in front of the corral and, much to his surprise, Lacey already stood by the fence. All five goats ate from her hand. This stroke of luck would gain him a time advantage if he could only get it to work out.

"Grab a collar, will you?" He snatched a lead line from the toolbox. Her expression held a question until he hustled over and snapped the line to the goat's collar. He pointed to the next candidate as he forced the gate open and led his captive out. Three goats later, he savored the cooperation as he returned for the last billy. Lacey held the adult goat tight but the kid scampered out of the corral to nibble the yard grass.

Wray clicked the lead line on and Lacey followed alongside toward the trailer where he rough-handled the animal inside. The kid skittered by and he gave a whistle. Hank launched on a search-and-rescue mission in front of the truck. Lacey opened the passenger door and before Wray could put a boot out to block the option, the kid leapt inside. Once settled on the seat mid-bench, it began to lick the gearshift. His helper shot him an eyebrow-heavy "take that" look and got in beside her little hoofed friend. The dog plopped on its haunches right outside the passenger-side door.

Wray ran for the back door. "Be right back."

"Grab my purse, will you?"

He crossed the sunroom into the kitchen, pulled the junk drawer open, and tucked a few trinkets for the children in his pocket. When a bakery tray of mini-muffins beckoned to him, he grabbed them, tapped his hat on, and backtracked. He stopped to assess her pile of belongings, a real no-man's land. He took the pink cowgirl hat and slid his arm through the purse strap. A well-landed boot kick on the screen door sent them on their way in record time.

~

Lacey held her hand out for his muffin paper and he surrendered it without eye contact. They passed through Mount Hope where the terrain pitched a fit of small hills and odd hummocks that the road had to traverse. She offered the paper to the baby goat that ate it with relish. The dog whimpered under her feet so she gave it a head-pat in appeasement.

Now that he'd enjoyed the bribe of her muffins, some candid confession might be in order. "Perhaps you could have mentioned that you intended to part ways with the goats before I got so attached." She looked straight ahead.

"Wren needs the money. Plus, it won't hurt me to lighten up for a while… until I get the farm back under me," Wray replied. "She isn't doing too well right now."

"*She* isn't doing well?" Incredulous over his perspective, her tone gave her away. "Should I sit here and pretend that I don't know your mortgage is heading for default?"

"No, ma'am," he insisted, staring at the road. "First off—I don't believe in pretense. Second, I'm allowing something else to have priority right now because of the dire circumstance it involves. Guess I need to tell you why we're having the fundraiser today, in all fairness. Must have gotten myself a little sidetracked last night but I sure meant to talk about it."

Now that he approached the truth of the matter, she relaxed her attitude a smidge. Her hand left the goat's back and found his arm. The corner of his eyes crinkled in response but he still seemed lost in a personal wrangle of some sort. Blame the highway, though traffic at this hour didn't exist.

"My eleven-year-old niece Pleasance is battling for her life," Wray confessed. "It's gone on about eighteen months—all uphill. Next month the chemo ends so the doctor wants to reevaluate where we are. Wren just takes it day-by-day, but I can see the toll on her. With Josiah gone, there was no health insurance when this hit, so we're raising money to help with her medical expenses."

She had to be pointed now, in case he thought to spare her the whole truth. "And what about the money diverted from your River Ranch mortgage?"

"It paid for the last series of treatments." He shook his head. "Now that I've sold the cattle, I've got some extra padding. My deal with Wren is that I'll pull out of the financial backing next month in time to redeem the mortgage from default. To me, though, it all hinges on what the doctor says next month."

A gritty emotion coursed through her veins, one she didn't even recognize, as though his circumstance accosted her safe-and-secure core convictions. Remorse bubbled up out of the fray and the urge to say something conciliatory weighed her thoughts.

"Wray, let me say I'm sorry. Sorry for the hardship your family has experienced and even more sorry how I walked right into it with the Notice of Default, not knowing your circumstance." She bit her lip before she fully incriminated her alter ego, the callous business woman.

He shook his head.

"You were just doing your job…"

"No, I've been too out-of-touch with people…with the things that truly matter. I don't think God will allow me to gloss over the heart-hurt behind the circumstance any longer."

His gaze strayed her way for the briefest moment, a glimmer of mischief in his eyes. "Oh? I like having a personal advocate in the bank's back office."

Her thoughts ricocheted down several trails of financial relief she'd contemplated for him. "I'm afraid my role hasn't had the least appearance of advocacy to date." When her train of thought went too far down that track, the touch of his hand brought her back into the present.

He squeezed her fingers. "No, but it will. When the right opportunity comes, you will."

Lacey added her right hand atop his to form a silent pact. Beyond reason, Wray believed in her. Now if only she could protect the trust and stitch it to her heart with gossamer threads.

~

Wray pulled past the mud pit that stretched between the highway and downtown Yoder. He allowed the truck to advance at a creep past half a dozen men fastening a perimeter rope around the tractor pull area. Two small sections of bleachers had been hauled in to flank the main viewing area and four tractors had already lined up to enter the competition. A quarter hour short of eight o'clock, they had arrived early and that somehow energized him. "Wow. Things are already hopping here."

"Tell me what I'm looking at." Lacey rolled her window down.

The smell of fresh cut hay floated into the cab and relaxed him as he searched for his designated spot. "This mud run hosts the tractor pull. I should mention that the locals allow themselves the luxury of tractors for their farm work even though they shun other modern conveniences. Living set-apart from technology draws a fine line, one Dad claimed he could never find."

"I bet they keep the competition friendly here, without the boast of bragging rights, I mean." She tossed a wave out to greet the team. A bearded man returned the good-natured greeting as the truck advanced into downtown. A couple of food vendors arrived early into town square and had begun to unfold their booths. Wray spotted a red bandana tied atop a wooden stake beyond the mown lawn and nosed the truck toward it. He scrutinized the layout. "Here's our spot."

"The goats will certainly love the tall grass even though my skirt won't." She patted the kid goat between them as it licked the radio knobs.

"I appreciate you honoring their modest customs today." He nodded down the length of her skirt. "You'll find that time truly slows down here. Mom always cherished that aspect of coming home for visits. Dad couldn't get over the feeling that they held something against him for taking her away, so he just tried to work hard to earn their favor."

"That's a world without grace." She rolled the window all the way down. The dog whined, unable to see from its post in the floorboard.

"Well—here's some grace. We have a tree for partial shade." He pointed out a rounded-crown tree standing on the meadow's edge. "It's a mulberry, I think. Though it may be too early for eating, I'm sure the womenfolk already have a claim staked for making jelly."

"When will we see Wren?"

"Sooner than later. Let's get this playpen up and then we'll stroll over before we put the animals inside. Her house isn't far." As he met Lacey at her door with a lead line for the kid goat, the dog began cutting circles around the truck in hyped anticipation. He motioned toward the tree before he grabbed the first fence bundle. Once he hefted it onto his shoulder, he followed her toward the tree.

Her interaction with the goat offered some

entertainment along the way. Predictable in its lack of cooperation, it stopped to eat the first long blades in its path and she had to gently coax it toward the tree, hooves dragging.

He dropped his load in the grass. "Now you see why we fence instead of staking them out," By the time he doubled back for the second enclosure, she had the first fence unrolled. "Run grab my hammer from the toolbox, will you?"

"You bet." She gathered her skirt to step out of the tall grass.

He eyed the tree and tried to project where their customers would approach so he could angle the enclosure for optimum exposure. After he had unfurled the second pen, he righted the first fence stake. The hammer soon dangled beside his hand.

"You don't want me to do the honors, trust me," she joked. "Let me hold the stake and you hammer."

"Now that's real pressure. I'm getting ready to introduce you to my sister and I dare not take you over all black and blue from hammer strikes."

"Oh, I'm sure you wouldn't hurt a flea...on purpose." She pulled her hair back into a ponytail and tapped on her hat. She grabbed the stake from him and set it in position.

He tweaked it toward vertical with a wink. On her nod, he tapped the top with an efficient stroke and repeated several times until he considered it set.

"Are we going for circular here?"

"Maybe more of a rough-hewn circle." He stood to move one post length down. Once she'd planted the next stake further out, he caught her gaze and rewarded her with a wry smile. "Watch out, Bank Lady—I think your country is showing." Beneath the pink hat brim, appreciation flashed in her green eyes, which made him refocus before the hammer went wayward under his forceful misdirection.

~

Lacey stood on the steps of a prim, narrow porch as Wray rapped his knuckles on the screen door. Not waiting for a reply, he pulled the flimsy frame open and stepped inside. She studied the flowerbeds that flanked the modest house and imagined the wispy color blocks as a stained glass mosaic that surrounded the porch like a halo. Sounds from the kitchen echoed through a nearby window and the faint aroma of cooked chicken wafted across the rail.

Wray's deep voice rumbled up from the back hall and was countered by a feminine response, followed by a raucous greeting by a child. Lacey bowed her head and smiled. No need to wonder what his sister's family meant to the lonesome rancher. She had a sudden urge to join the reunion and share the feel-good. Had it not been for the illness inside, she would have. In seconds, the screen door parted and a petite woman stepped out, her face careworn beyond her young years.

She wiped her flour-coated hands on her apron. "I'm Wren, Wray's sister," she said. "So great of you to come help today, as Wray and I both need a hand."

"Can't think of any place I'd rather be. I'm Lacey Woodhouse."

A child's laughter rolled through the screen and kindled a spark in the woman's eyes. "Wray's always good medicine around here."

"Oh, I can believe that. All he has is the kid goat back home and I play with it more than he does."

That brought an all-too-brief laugh from the weary mother. "My brother works too much, which is why I'm grateful you're in the picture to balance him out a little."

Wray appeared at the door with a young boy wrapped around his neck like a human scarf. "Lacey, meet my nephew Josh." He butted his head against the boy's midsection. The preschooler smiled around the plastic whistle in his mouth, a gift from his uncle, no doubt.

Wren knitted her brow. "Try not to make him swallow that thing, Wray. We don't have time for the hospital today."

"We don't have time for the hospital any day." He disappeared with an exaggerated bounce away from the front door.

Wren wrung her hands. "You'll come over to help set up lunch, won't you?"

Lacey resisted the urge to hold hands and touched the sleeve of her cotton shift instead. "Trust me, as soon as your brother and his goats don't need me, I'll be back. I might have to wash the herd off me once I get here, though."

A wave of relief washed over Wren's face as she pulled the door open and disappeared with a gracious nod.

Left alone on the porch, Lacey overheard Wray ask to see his niece. A low-pitched conversation ensued. Two women with white aprons atop their cotton dresses walked by, trying to hide their furtive glances. Maybe her sequined sandals didn't pass as the norm around here.

The reverie of the quaint setting shattered the

second Wray's boot shoved the screen door open. He huffed out of the house, slid his hat in place, and stomped down the short flight of steps before he seemed to remember her.

She followed without a word and jogged as necessary to catch up. The morning's calm began to filter back over her. She shifted closer and grazed his shoulder with hers. "Dear Lord, we stride into this glorious day with the knowledge that you hold us in the palm of your hand. Don't let us feel like outsiders here, as we're all your children. We ask you to place a healing hand on Pleasance, as she truly needs your touch today. In the infinite power of Jesus' name, we pray."

"Don't say amen," Wray said, his tone full of hurt. His hand slid into hers and their fingers interlaced to claim the prayer together.

The way their last prayer had ended flushed a heat wave up her neckline. There's no way that display of affection could happen out here on the picket fence-lined streets of Quaint-ville.

He gave her a sideways glance from under his hat brim. "I'll have to owe you one." A dimple appeared for an infinitesimal moment.

She gave his fingers a squeeze to accept his terms for the private loan. Though she'd spent every day of her short career in banking, she had never received a credit that made her stomach flip before. The day would have to improve before she could call in that loan, and she fully intended to call it in.

Chapter 8

The benchmark of midmorning passed and Wray wiped his forehead in frustration. All this chitchat with the locals had produced only a handful of bids. The tractor pull seemed to have a lock on the crowd. He'd have to let Lacey go soon which meant he'd forfeit his attention magnet, as most of the menfolk seemed to hook up in lengthy conversations with her at the bid table. He heard the chronic complaint of a dozen Plymouth Rock pullets housed in with the goats and decided it was high time to do something about it.

In six steps his legs pressed against the back bumper of his truck where he lifted out a nearly empty bag of cracked corn. With his back turned to the cheers from the tractor pull, he detected motion along the meadow's edge. A solitary figure led a calf toward his station. Heartened by the possibility of an unexpected donor, he stepped back toward the enclosure and flung a handful of corn at the clucky complainers.

Two men and a teenage boy left the bid table so he worked around the circle pen until he fell in conversational distance. Another handful of corn spattered around the tree trunk and three of the pullets followed him.

Lacey stepped toward the fence and he felt her presence. "Something tells me I should go soon." She removed her hat to tuck a few loose strands back into her ponytail.

He turned half toward her, rolled the feedbag closed, and tossed it under the table. "Soon. I want you to meet somebody first."

"Okay, Wray. Seems like everybody wants the chickens, not the goats." The kid goat worked its way around the tree trunk to the dismay of the pullets, which gave up ground with attitude. She reached out and scratched the goat's rump.

Wray realized the fallacy of her comment. "Maybe not everybody," he replied with a slow wink. He dusted the corn off his hands and wiped them across his back pockets as a figure dressed in overalls appeared at the far end of the pen, calf in tow. Lacey straightened as the man drew closer and Wray stepped toward him.

"Luke, it's good to see you." Wray extended his hand, which the man readily accepted. "This is a friend of mine from town, Lacey Woodhouse. Lacey, this is Luke Yost, a long-time friend of the family."

"Ma'am." He tipped his hat while his gaze dropped to his own boots.

"So nice to meet you," Lacey replied.

"Nice piece of cow hide you're pulling around," Wray added.

Luke's face warmed with demur pride and his eyes

gleamed. "Thought we could put her up for bid today and see what she'd bring, for Wren, of course. If you don't think she'd be too much trouble, that is."

"A generous act seldom translates into trouble," Wray assured him.

Lacey touched his elbow. "Something this exquisite at auction needs to have a minimum bid set, Wray." She stepped around the men and began to stroke the calf.

The calf's skin twitched at the domestic contact. Wray experienced a jolt of jealousy that soon hooked a smile in his cheek. "Good idea. A Guernsey calf holds a lot of promise beyond milk production, Luke. What say we put two Ben Franklins down for the bottom line?"

The farmer turned to the creature as if the answer was written down its flank. "Maybe a buck-fifty. I don't want to be walking this calf back home come evening. Wren needs the money and I can't hardly find a way she'll let me help her otherwise."

Wray worked his lips together dealing with the last confession, as he'd been in a similar spot, too. "This is mighty generous of you, Luke." His throat pinched with emotion that someone else could possibly be sensitive to her needs.

Luke swept his hat off to mop his brow. "Well, once God puts it on your heart, you can hardly do otherwise."

"How about we stake her out at the edge of the shade and let her choose the direction?" Wray indicated the meadow beyond the pen's fence. Luke nodded and followed him.

Lacey stepped to the bid table and pulled a sheet out to start the paperwork. "Does the calf have a name?" Lacey paused her pen in midair.

"Her name is Lovie," Luke replied.

Wray could tell Lacey found the moniker endearing and enjoyed the transformation in her countenance. That made his next move all the harder.

"Luke, how about you trust me to get Lovie staked out? I really need to get Lacey over to Wren's so she can help her get lunch ready. Could you walk her over for me?"

Lacey seemed ready to object but the answer came too quickly.

"Be honored to. Anything for Wren. You know that, Wray." He handed off the lead line and pulled the stake-out pin from his back pocket, ready to be shed of the responsibility.

Hands full, Wray could only catch Lacey now with his gaze, so he made it count. "Go be a blessing. And don't forget to bring a plate back for little ole me once the lunch rush is over."

Her mouth puckered as she bent to place the new bid sheet face out on the table and matched it with a pen. "Well that depends. Are you a paying customer, mister?"

His lips relaxed into a coy smile. "My money's right here in my left pocket if you're game enough to come fetch it." He gave his shoulder a shrug.

Luke cleared his throat and offered his elbow as she froze over the bid table. "Let's save the lady's honor and consider your credit good at Wren's booth." A hint of good-natured humor filled his eyes.

Lacey took his arm with a gesture that looked like a hybrid curtsey. "Thank you, Luke. Now Wray. Don't get too lonely here under the mulberry tree all by yourself."

"No worries, as I have Lovie here to keep me company." He lifted the lead line that led to a rather inert mass on its far end.

"Best of luck with that." Luke settled his hat in place as they strolled out of the shade.

Wray weighed his obligations in the moment as he tugged the calf to its interim destination. He corkscrewed the stake in place with more force than necessary. The most eligible bachelor in the village had just walked off with his gal. When Luke laughed, its ripple hit him low, about the level of a cow's knee. "You'd better sell," he muttered. The calf blinked its long lashes and went for the new plot of shaded grass.

~

Lacey traced the street front with her gaze as the first white picket fence popped into view along the corner. "So Luke, how long have you been a family friend?"

"Oh, we played together as kids since our farm sits next door to the Bontrager's place," Luke replied, his gaze focused on the row of tightly tucked houses. "Our chicken coop became the school, the clubhouse, or whatever Wren wanted it to be. I was always happy to play along, but Wray only wanted to ride our pony."

She noticed her escort's fondness for talking about Wray's sister. "That figures. But it seems like Wren would let you help out more since you two go back so far."

"Maybe you haven't gotten a good glimpse of the Benson's hard-headed trait yet," he replied. The admission pulled a half-smile onto his face.

She chuckled and nodded to acknowledge her

acquaintance with the character flaw.

Luke stubbed his toe into the gravel roadway. "Seriously though, God's putting her through a refiner's fire, first with Josiah's tragedy at the granary and now Pleasance's ailment. My prayer begs that she comes out fashioned into the silver chalice he intends. And sooner is better Lord, if you're listening."

"I know Wray appreciates your concern, Luke, even if he can't find the words to say so."

"He's like a brother to me. No need for us to over-talk it."

"Can you tell me about Pleasance's ailment? Wray won't put a name on it. Like if he speaks it, it somehow makes it more real."

They passed three houses before any answer came. "Leukemia. I never tried to pray something away so hard in my life. She's so young and lively, playful like Wren was. But the chemo's been a real energy-robber."

Lacey sensed a heart-tug to bridge the gap between the two. "Wray told me Wren has learned to take it one day at a time. She won't be preoccupied by this forever, Luke."

"I suppose not, but it already feels like an eternity, even from outside her picket fence," he replied, his gaze downcast.

Lacey searched for something relevant that might help the man gain some favor, though her knowledge of the family was limited. The chic nook flashed to mind and she came up with a nugget to offer.

"Here's a little something I found out about Wren. She likes to collect little tokens from nature. I slept up in her hayloft girls' club last night so Wray and I could get here early enough, and I saw her collection. Maybe that could help you bribe your way through her gate someday."

"Thanks for the insider's tip." His eyes crinkled at the corners. "Any advantage might make a difference in wearing down her resistance."

When he halted, she recognized the flowerbeds around the front porch. "Duty calls," she admitted, sorry to surrender the conversation because of the needless separation she sensed between the two. A reassuring thought came to mind and she felt compelled to share it. "Don't forget whose trusted hand opens and closes the secret gate of the heart." She figured he would only look at his boots in acknowledgment and was duly surprised at the direct gaze of gratitude that met hers.

"Lacey? Thank goodness above," Wren called from the screen door. "I was about ready to send Josh for you. Morning, Luke."

"Morning, Wren. Blame it on me. I brought Wray a calf to auction off but we ran a little late due to some split-hoofed stubbornness."

Her face softened momentarily with complex appreciation, which quickly shifted to something more urgent. "Luke, if I don't get that canopy raised in the next half-hour, Lacey and I will have to serve lunch under the broiling sun."

"Well, that won't do, will it, Wren? I'll have a go at putting it up for you. Should I pull a wagon?"

"No need. It's already down on the front porch of the General Store. All you have to do is set it up."

"How about sending Josh out to help me?" he pressed. "You've got your helper now. Besides, that kitchen work is for girls."

Lacey saw the protective mother clench her teeth until her jaw flexed as she weighed her options, a gesture her brother already held the patent on.

"All right. I suppose he could help you line up the poles," Wren replied. Her eyes locked onto his as if to reinforce her reluctance and he tipped his hat as though to convey his worthiness.

Lacey stepped toward the porch with a subtle smile at the breakthrough. "I think I might have just heard a gate hinge squeak," she said under her breath as she passed him.

"Let me get his shoes on and I'll send him right out," Wren offered. "And Luke, about donating the calf."

"Don't mention it, Wren. You and Wray would do the same for me and you know it," Luke replied, his gaze soft and compassionate.

His admission brought some color to the young mother's drained face as they regarded one another. "Your lunch will be on me then." Wren fidgeted and shifted her apron down on her hips. "Come by late when I'm not so busy."

Lacey followed her hostess into the house, but not before she managed to raise a brow in Luke's direction in told-you-so assertion as she reported to chicken noodle duty, a real promotion.

~

Wray counted no fewer than seven farmers around the pen's perimeter. Now things were moving forward. The tractor pull had generated its new champion and all the spectators had dispersed around downtown. In the distance he could see that the food vendors were thick with business. He whispered a sentence prayer that a fair share of it would pass Wren's way. A heavyset woman demonstrated strong interest in the flock of pullets so her husband ambled toward him at the bid table.

"Where's the chicken sheet?"

Wray tapped the pencil on the right sheet. Something told him to hold his peace and let the man ruminate over the top bid amount. That took longer than he thought.

"You Miriam Bontrager's boy?" the man asked without looking up.

"Yes sir. I'm Wray Benson." He knew the community continued to use his mother's maiden name, but he wouldn't let it rile him the way his father had. The man circled his pen tip over the page like he was warming up his mark. Maybe his distinct bushy brow should have clued Wray to his identity but his memory couldn't come up with it. Finally, the man made his indication for the bid and dropped the writing utensil.

"Sorry for your loss," he mumbled, so faint that Wray could barely make it out.

"Appreciate that, sir," he managed. "And thank you for the bid." As the man made his way back to his wife, Wray turned the bid sheet and his gaze landed on the amount, double the previous bid and he wanted all of the pullets. Encouraged that he might have just sold the poultry, he focused on deciphering the name. It looked like Glazner to him, a name that sounded somewhat familiar. Why his mind kept linking the grain elevator to the name escaped him. He'd have to ask Wren once Heritage Days wound down.

Several new parties stepped into the livestock area. One man garnered several slaps on the back, unusual for the typically reserved community. Wray wandered down the cusp of the fence under the pretense of straightening fence stakes. Once he overheard the blow-by-blow of the record mud drag, he figured out the fellow must be the new champion of the tractor pull. With such a sizable prize pot, Wray knew the winner carried a couple hundred dollars of surplus spending power.

He waited to catch their conversation in a lull. "Need a good milk cow around your place? It's a Yost Guernsey. That's a strong line."

"You don't say?" The man stroked his beard. "Worth a look, I reckon."

Wray indicated the calf's location on the far side of the mulberry tree and allowed the man to lead. He made a pit stop at the bid table where he paused to read the fundraiser flyer that bore an adorable photo of Pleasance cropped into the center. Finally, he stepped over toward the staking pin and eyed the calf.

Wray's sales pitch came short and sweet. "She's only three months old and promises to be a good producer." He rubbed his right hand across the calf's squared hindquarter.

"Reckon so," the man replied from deep contemplation. "We lost two cows from our milking herd this past winter, so we're short right now."

"Tough winter all the way around," he admitted, his thoughts focused on his niece. "Good Lord willing, we'll get it turned around this summer."

Silent now, the potential bidder stepped around the far side of the calf and gave it his full assessment. Without further exchange, the man returned to the table, recorded his bid and pulled out his pocket watch to gauge how much longer his bid would have to hold. "See you at five o'clock then." He reached across the table to shake hands. "You know, one day that outgoing tide's bound to turn."

Wray ventured a glance at the bid sheet and took heart to believe. "Maybe today even." Moved by the generosity of the tractor champion, he struggled to regain a foothold of respect for the community. As the man walked away, he made a quick tally between the bid sheets and exhaled. His ribs seemed to touch front-to-back, so he began to wonder who had hijacked his lunch.

~

Lacey mopped the table with a wet tea towel as Wren disappeared around the corner headed for the bank drop box with Luke as her vigilant escort. With a quick check of the vat of chicken noodles, she estimated enough food remained for the men to split for their courtesy lunches. When she looked up, a stern-faced young woman stood before her.

She scanned Lacey's frame with steely eyes. "You some friend of Wren's?" She popped a hand on her ample hips.

Lacey dropped the towel. "I'm a friend of her brother, Wray."

A not-so-pleased look flitted across the woman's face. "We call him Look-Away-Wray at the bakery." Her expression came nothing short of gloating. "He comes by every time he's in town. A girl doesn't need much imagination to wonder why."

"Maybe he's soft on your cinnamon rolls." Lacey emphasized her point with a forced smile.

The woman enjoyed a belly laugh at her expense,

which dissipated into sourness. She squinted her eyes, accentuating her puffy cheeks. "Wray belongs here in our community."

"No—he belongs at River Ranch." Her tone steady, Lacey made the claim sound like an absolute.

"Not after God takes it away from him." The woman lowered her chin as though she spoke with higher authority. With a saucy pivot, she spun away from the table and disappeared into the general store, which left a mess of a different sort to mop up.

Chapter 9

Wray straightened his bent legs from the top step of Wren's front porch. "I never thought the day would have twenty-two hundred written on it."

Luke stared at the flowerbed. "Good crowd today."

"Generous crowd, you included," Wray replied. Sounds of pots being put away clanked from the front window as Josh appeared down the sidewalk with a couple of his buddies. "Don't go so far that I can't see you," Wray called to him in warning as they sped past for a ball.

"You've been on kid duty all the live-long day," Luke teased.

"Every kind of kid but the one that's on my mind most. Wren says she's having a bad day, but that I might be able to see her before we leave." He scratched his cheek and tried not to be down about it. The comment about the tide turning came back to him and he thought he might like to put that to prayer and see if

God might be open to a change of direction.

"I'd like to court Wren," Luke said, his fingertips pressed together. "Since your dad's gone, I'm asking you, Wray. I could see she needed me today, and for once she let me help her. I'm not ready to go back down the road to my place and pretend that moment didn't happen. Could you… speak to her on my behalf? Feels like I'm not making any headway on my own."

Wray looked at his boyhood friend and recognized the sincerity in his eyes, even though he pretty much knew what consternation he'd up against with his sister. A positive ploy came to him as a second thought.

"I'd be glad to, Luke. But don't be surprised if somebody hasn't beaten me to it, as I think you gained a friend in Lacey today."

"She's a good listener. Had me figured out in short order and gave me some tips to get on Wren's good side."

Wray laughed and caught sight of Josh coming around the corner lot minus the friends.

"Maybe I ought to get the boy back over here," Luke added.

Wray stood and tried to shake the ache off from being on his feet all day. "Go ahead. I'll test the waters and see if I can gain audience with my niece now." When Luke gave a shrill whistle, he got an instant reaction of obedience from the preschooler, which made an impression on him. "Yeah, you've sure got a way with that boy, all right." Wray placed a hand on his friend's shoulder as he passed behind him to go inside. From the living room, he could hear the women mention trust as they worked in the kitchen. He popped around the corner and interrupted to state his case.

"Night's going to be falling soon and Lacey needs to get her goats back to River Ranch," he said. "Can you trust me with a quick visit with Pleasance before we head out?"

Wren dropped her drying towel and scooted past him without a word.

He slid next to Lacey and thought he'd better make sure their promises had been covered. He turned the faucet on to wash up. "Have you said anything to her yet about opening up to Luke a little?"

"Why, indeed I have, Look-Away-Wray," she replied, her lips pulled tight.

"Where in the world did you hear that nickname?"

"I had a visitor at the booth after all the lunches were served when Wren did the bank drop. Guess she was biding her time until she could trap me alone."

"To do what exactly?" He sensed something had fallen out of balance. The soap foam made its way up his forearms as he scrubbed the livestock smell from his hands.

"To stake her claim on you, if my intuition is properly functioning, which it is."

"You've definitely lost me now." He shoved his hands under for a final rinse.

"Well it starts with cinnamon rolls, and ends with you stopping by every time you're in town. That might get a woman's hopes up, say—if she lived in a place where eligible men came few and far between."

He borrowed her tea towel to dry his hands and then slapped his forehead as the pieces fell into place and the round-faced clerk at the town's bakery came to mind.

"Wray, guess we're ready for company back here,"

Wren called.

He stepped closer to Lacey and beamed an intimate message to her piercing green eyes. "Let's tackle this on the way home, as I don't want there to be any confusion. You own my goats now, after all, so we have to trust one another." A smile toyed with the corners of his mouth as he turned and strode down the hall to the back rooms.

Wren waited at the door to a pink bedroom that seemed far too short on cheeriness. She began to step away and let him gain entrance.

Wray caught her arm and held her beside him. "Don't make me have to reveal the dollar amount on what that calf brought today. Just let me ask that you give Luke some time and consideration for his… tenderness toward the family. That's all I ask."

"I already have my mind made up," she replied, "to do just that. Not because you say so, but because I feel it in my heart. What's left of the feelings in my heart, that is."

"Well maybe there's a fix for that waiting to happen, you never know. Leave Josh with Lacey for now and you two step away. Go for a walk or something."

"Goodness knows you're bossy, all of a sudden," she quipped. Her eyes spoke something different from her words.

He released her and took a protracted breath before he entered the room where someone dear waited for him. The cares of the day fell away as he came in and knelt by her bedside. The child turned to him, gaunt of face but with eyes full of love.

"How's my precious girl today?" No matter the

answer, he had her now and had to learn Wren's skill of taking it one day at a time. More than one doomsday clock was ticking which made it crystal clear that life wasn't meant to be lived like this.

~

With Wray a little too quiet when they pulled out of town, Lacey wanted to both give him room and get closer all at the same time. The day had been a mix of devotion and discovery, with ninety-nine percent of it heartening and wonderful. She had beaten down the specter of the possibility of Wray being interested in someone else, thanks to Wren's candid assessment of the situation. Still, Wray had wanted to clear the air, and she'd let him do it when the time felt right.

The truck slowed and the driver seemed distracted by the scenery. "Not in a hurry, are we?" He continued to look at the roadside.

"No, go ahead and detour, if you want to." She gazed ahead at a bridge railing. The truck soon nosed down a sandy road to where the tracks gave way to a solid stretch of sand.

He pulled beside a stand of trees and cut the ignition without a word of explanation. The dog shot out of the floorboard causing the kid goat some alarm. She managed to click the lead line in place and led it out her door to the sandy shore of the gently flowing river.

The sun had already dropped below the treetops, leaving only indirect light playing across the river's surface. Several ribbons of clear water flowed between expansive sand bars. The whole setting took on a dream-like quality. Maybe this was what he'd meant by taking her down to the river—not an analogy, but a literal visit to the water's edge. She kicked her shoes off to wade into the closest flow, while she knotted her skirt up on one side to keep its hem dry.

Hank barked upriver and she glanced over in time to see Wray throw a stick to fetch. Tethered to duty under the mulberry tree all day, the dog seemed like a puppy, wanting exercise and attention. The vitality of the water made her spring alive again, too.

The goat pulled toward an area of overgrown grass and she gave it as much line as possible before she surrendered to the river. At first, merely her legs were in the flow as she sat down on a raised bank. After a few minutes of partial immersion, she gave way to the full effect, keeping her head up on the sandbar with everything else submerged. The water's touch proved divine and life giving as it passed over her. Time stood still. Only the river moved.

After a while, she felt a strong tug on the goat's line. Wray's outline hovered over her. She relinquished the line to his care and shifted her shoulders in the sand. As the sun set, she lowered the brim of her hat to shield its last light. The next thing she knew, he knelt beside her.

His gaze held a far-away look but sincerity rested on his face. "Now you know why I have to go down to the river." His voice sounded smooth like the flowing water. "Next, I believe I owe you an amen from earlier today." He took her hat and tossed it in the sand. The river's scenery faded as he bent and administered the payment, sweet and savory at first touch and then deeper and questing before it ended.

The combined effect of water and man seemed to extract every ounce of worry from her heart, leaving only a separation of air around the heady desire for more. "Wow, I don't think I can take the two of you together for very long." Mesmerized, she sat up to break the spell.

He laughed at her professed weakness and handed her the pink hat as the goat tugged him uphill toward a stand of grass. "How about we walk up the river a piece so you can dry off before I put you back in my truck?"

Lacey stood and squeezed the excess water out of her skirt. The cool breeze on her skin lent its enjoyable prickle as dusk fell around them. "It's beautiful here. Is this the same river that flows past River Ranch?"

He hooked the lead line onto the trailer and left the goat in a grassy patch while the dog lunged ahead. "One and the same—the Arkansas. Only looks different here, thin like a ribbon."

She timed her next step to fall in with his. "You haven't taken me down to the river yet, like you promised that first day."

He paused for a few moments and looked into her eyes. When she loosened her ponytail, his hand came up and touched several strands as they blew across her shoulder. He stepped closer and his shadow engulfed her. "Maybe that's because you haven't been bad off enough to go down yet."

Lacey considered the prospect. Perhaps something beyond rejuvenation existed in the flow, a force more like restoration or even reconciliation. Whatever the fix, the river held the low point on the landscape so you had to come down to it before you could go back up healed.

"By the way, you don't see me looking away from you right now, do you?" His tone had turned velvety smooth. His hands found the curve of her shoulders and he moved even closer to assist with the answer. He blinked and his eyelashes painted a swath of candid intent across his face in the low light.

His meaning wrapped her heart like a bandage. "No. I don't see anyone looking away."

"Isn't that the way it's supposed to be between a man and a woman, open and honest?" He caught a few strands of loose hair and cleared them from her face.

Her answer wouldn't come in words as his silent magnetism pulled her in. She did the one thing she could do, barefoot in the sand. She tiptoed up and planted a kiss on his lips, every bit as full and succulent as a cinnamon roll in a bakery window. When he hummed with satisfaction, she ducked under his grasp and ran up the river. "I'm supposed to be letting my clothes dry, right?" She laughed and twirled on the sand bar as free as a shorebird.

He darted toward her as the dog barked at his heels. The first lightning bug claimed the sandbar nearby.

Lacey tried to capture it all in her heart. Immensely happy, she was falling for a kind-hearted rancher, such a wet-skinned, to-the-bone sensation that felt like nothing she'd ever experienced. This was really living.

~

The day started to hit him like a ton of bricks about the time the last goat found its way back into the corral. Wray cleaned out the truck cab, topping his hat with her pink one so he could carry more stuff inside. He left his door open with her purse balanced on the edge of his seat. "Let's go inside. I need to crash."

Of course, the worst part was that Lacey would have to head back to town, which left him dead tired and alone, his least favorite combination. Funny how the loneliness never seemed to matter before she showed up. He shook his head to clear the thought as he stepped into the sunroom off the rear of the house.

In the back porch light, he spotted her things strewn across the sofa and the stab went deeper. He struggled into the kitchen and popped the leftover muffins onto the counter. An armful of stuff found the top of the table and he tossed his hat on the far counter, like always. When he came out from the back hall, he found Lacey in the dining room, the light in the buffet refracting through tiny glass figurines that glinted onto her face.

She glanced up at him for a brief moment and then back at the buffet as though the colors brought a melancholy of sorts. "I'm not quite ready to go back to town living yet."

Something pressed on his heart like a crowbar against a bent nail and he closed the separation between them in short order. Their shoulders touched and her skin felt soft and cool. "So why go back when your chic nook is so spacious and accommodating?"

She leaned her head onto his shoulder, which seemed to assuage her sadness.

"Plus you have the goats. Now there's a real responsibility. Looks like you'll have to spend some time out here on the weekends to feed up and all." His words dropped into her hairline as he tried to make light while she came to grips with whatever dampened her spirit. "A goat can get real attached. Don't be fooled for a minute by their independent streak. No, ma'am. They're a needy bunch if you think about it. And that owlet trio will be gone in two months, tops. By end of summer, you'll find they've flown the coop without so much as a look back."

He stopped his nonsense long enough to check her response and found the somber mood seemed to have dried up. Dusting her hair with a kiss, he held her back to get a look into her eyes. The green pools sparkled with sincerity. His hand trickled down and met hers as the leaden feeling of fatigue hit hard. "Let's find a place to sit down so I can get off my feet." He pulled her toward the front of the house and opened the door to get a breeze drawing through.

"How about the porch swing? Meet you out there in a minute." She took a detour down the back hall.

Wray pulled the screen door open. A small card fell out of the crack and he bent to retrieve it. A surveyor's business card had been hand-marked with the day's date and the letters REO on the back. A lump formed in his throat at the thought of his rural kingdom being sized up for relinquishment. He put the card on the end table and banged out of the screen door into the night air. As his mind raced around the foreclosure, his thoughts settled on the gaunt child's face in the pink room that he had seen earlier. In the dim light of human effort, her struggle made his monetary wrangle seem inconsequential by comparison.

Chapter 10

The little church in Maize was originally brick that sprawled into several vinyl-sided additions, which Lacey took as a sign that the Holy Spirit actively moved in the local congregation. Families arrived together and several little girls skipped into the education wing. A couple of joggers passed, heedless of the property, and reminded her that many souls were not choosing to surrender their morning in affirmation of God and his almighty power. In her estimation, life was a little too fragile to proceed without acknowledgement of the divine.

"I'm in the cowboy class." Wray thumped his Bible to his side. "Hope you don't mind being a minority."

"Men outnumber women two-to-one at the bank," she replied. "You'd think I was born to be underserved."

"Not in the eyes of Jesus." He took her hand in his. "Our young adult class is a mixed group studying the

Old Testament prophets. Lots of moaning and groaning going on back then."

"Sounds like Jeremiah," she replied. A man appeared inside the door they approached and the door pushed open at his insistence.

Wray shook his hand and he nodded at her as they exchanged greetings. The entrance hall narrowed down to a host of doorways and Wray stopped at the third one and motioned her in. Two semicircles of chairs faced the front of the room where a wipe-off board had been filled with neat handwritten notes under the heading "Why We Should Lament." They settled in the back row near another couple and Wray opened his Bible to the Book of Lamentations.

"I didn't want to scare you away by telling you we were done with the weeping prophet and had moved on to the collection of his major gripes," he joked. "You could say that I'm living out some of this down-and-out stuff right now, so I make myself pay attention in case there's an easy fix."

His smirked-up grin generated a compassionate response inside her heart and she flashed him a look that made sure he knew she was on his side.

A man made his way around the group passing out the lecture outline. He smiled and gave Wray two copies. "How's your niece?" He paused in front of them.

"Yesterday wasn't her best day, but the fundraiser had strong results," he replied. "Gene, this is a friend of mine, Lacey Woodhouse. Lacey, meet our teacher, Gene Weston."

"Glad to have you in class today," he replied. "Wray lives so far out I was beginning to wonder if he had any friends."

"A business trip out turned to pleasure when we met." She took a paper from him.

"Funny how God works like that, isn't it?" He nodded and continued his distribution.

"Yeah, funny." Wray took her hand in his.

Lacey pretended to study the handout but all she could think about were all the years she had attended church by herself while everyone else seemed to pair up and graduate to the couples' class. Maybe this chance meeting represented salvation of another sort. She had to admit that it had a good feel to it, like a letting go.

"Let's get class started and see where this lament thing leads," Gene posed.

"The ditch!" replied a wisecracker on the other side of the room. Laughter filled the air, which soon included the chortle of the class leader as he shuffled his papers on the lectern.

"Nothing wrong with low—as long as you know to look up for help," he replied.

Lacey settled in for an interesting session on desperation, as though she could see its tangible specter on the horizon.

~

A tiny organ played the final note of prelude, and a mixed-age choir took the stage, as Wray grew restless for the service to begin. Maybe it had been the announcement about the upcoming Father's Day celebration that cut into the quick, or perhaps the Sunday school lesson had struck a little too close for comfort. Despite his uneasiness, Lacey seemed to be enjoying her morning, which anchored him more than he cared to admit.

"Before we begin, please turn and extend the hand of fellowship," the pastor directed.

Wray turned toward her and enjoyed the warmth of faith borne on her gaze. When she mouthed "thank you,'" his tenseness loosened a bit. Turning toward the aisle, he found the little sparkplug of a greeter that typically met him at the door.

"Morning, Miss Cora." He bent to shake her arthritic hand.

"Don't just morning me, you big lunker," she replied. "Tell me who this dark-haired beauty is so I can say hello."

He leaned back so the two ladies could meet but couldn't get the introduction started.

"I'm Cora Clark, honey. I've been here since Methuselah resigned and hope to be here until the Lord comes back or takes me up!"

"I'm Lacey Woodhouse, Miss Cora. It's nice to meet you this morning."

"I'll be at the front door when you come out so I'll get the skinny on you then." Cora smacked the bulletin onto her palm and shuffled to the back for latecomers.

Wray looked up at the pastor as he tried to restore order from the pulpit and cleared his throat for the singing portion of worship. When Lacey leaned into him, he turned to catch her message as the organ fired up and the choir stood.

"Looks like somebody has a fan club."

He gave her a quick patronizing smile and pointed to the order of service inserted into the bulletin as the choir lit into the chorus. By the end of the first praise song, he sensed the calm presence of the Holy Spirit and sang the second song with renewed vigor. Lacey's voice crested with his and even that blend seemed to bring him added peace. When they resumed their seats, his mood had taken a right turn. He looked forward to the sermon with great anticipation as the pastor took his place in front of the congregation.

"Hope is the thing with feathers." He glanced up through the rims of his glasses. "Especially if the feather happens to have dropped from the dove of the Holy Spirit, God's designated encourager." When Lacey elbowed his ribs, he broke his study of the bulletin's outline to regard her written message.

She had scratched out part of the sermon title and written across it "Hope is the thing for the faltering" and underneath her pen revealed what was on her list of personal struggles. The first line read "Pleasance." The second entry was "mortgage default." The third and last entry hovered on her pen point in hesitation, but soon appeared. It read "unhappy at work."

Number three represented new territory for conversation, but Wray determined it would get some attention when the discussion could be more casual, like in a meadow of daisies where cares could just blow away. He slid his hand atop hers as the sermon unfolded.

~

"Never knew I would like perimeter checks." Lacey swung his hand in hers. She had changed into shorts and sneakers after church at Wray's insistence. A loose belt made of a lazy daisy chain clung to her hips as a host of insects scattered with their every step. "What are these tiny purple ones called?"

"That's false alfalfa. And these tiny daisy fleabane will last all summer but your favorite bouquet flowers are on their way out, I'm afraid. That's the short life of a wildflower."

"Will July be just as beautiful as June?"

"Even more so—with blue wild indigo in the meadow and fireworks of coreopsis along the ditch banks. Once blooming season starts on the prairie, it keeps going like a long parade."

She had to think about that for a few seconds, how something so enjoyable could be gone in a matter of weeks. An idea came to her and she thought it had some merit.

"Maybe I could capture these prairie blooms in stained glass and freeze their beauty in time so more people could enjoy them." She squared her fingertips to entrap the scenery as though the art show had already begun.

He laughed and plucked a nearby daisy to offer her. "I think you just found a new inspiration, Miss Woodhouse. Now maybe you'll come back out here more often."

"As often as the wildflowers change." A scan of the meadow revealed countless blooms among the grass. Shouldn't the cattle be eating away this abundance? "Is this pasture grazed?"

"Not right now, as I just sold off the herd. We usually take the cattle off by mid-July so I'm only a few weeks early. Dad called it the Henley pasture, as he bought it from my neighbor's father years ago. I prefer to call it the West pasture because, well—the Henleys don't deserve the mention. Let's just say that the current occupant isn't as reputable as former generations."

As he stopped to tighten a fence strand that

drooped, Lacey processed the information. "Is the wheat on the other side of the driveway yours, Wray?" Though she tried, she couldn't get the layout of the land straight in her mind.

"Yeah, all one hundred and twenty acres of it. Well, it's really two fields of sixty, and together they echo the size of this pasture like mirror images. The rest of the three hundred and twenty acres includes the house, the orchard, and the barnyard, plus the lower pasture where I keep my horse down by the river. We'll come back up through there so you can get a peek at some of my secret places, as long as you don't rat me out to those bank people."

"Don't worry." Her tone held a little more vinegar than necessary.

He tucked the daisy into the neckline of her t-shirt and tapped her chin up with his fingers. "Want to talk about number three on your faltering hope list?"

Something about his unassuming question and the beauty of the setting made her want to open up about her workplace. Thoughts tumbled until she found an adequate starting point. "I don't know what I thought it was going to be like Wray, not to sound too much like a disillusioned teenager." She lengthened her stride to keep up with his. "I was good in math so when my college advisor recommended a degree in finance, I agreed and dreamed of banking where we worked for the people, you know, kept their money safe and helped make their dreams come true." She paused for a breath but couldn't stop the sarcastic laugh that issued forth. She shook her head and tucked an errant strand of hair behind her ear.

"Not helping too many people where you're

stationed in foreclosures, I'm guessing."

"Oh, no. Quite the opposite. We seem to make the foreclosure process a lot like leading cattle to the slaughterhouse. The whole thing is cut-and-dried, the countdown schedule, the next step that thumbscrews the property owner, the impossibility of recovery and eventually, the forfeiture of the property. It's all a downward spiral, which makes me have to go into this fake aggressive mode where I deliver the bad news to people and leave without looking them in the eye. And my boss, Mr. Odom, seems to even derive pleasure from other people's losses—which strikes me as twisted and sick."

"That's why he sits in the power seat, but that doesn't make it the right approach."

She made a guttural noise in disgust and twisted the stem off her daisy. "Something almost seems wrong there. Almost nobody pulls out once the Fidelis Bank forecloses. My friend Julie told me that we have the highest foreclosure rate in the state. Mr. Odom says it's because I do my job so well. Why doesn't he just heap coals on my head?"

"I fully intend to pull out of this foreclosure, so you can share in my victory when River Ranch breaks free and clear," Wray assured her. "I guess that makes mine the atypical case. Have you ever thought of hopping the fence to be an advocate for the folks heading for financial trouble? Or is it too lucrative for the bank the way it is now?"

She gave the thought some careful consideration, as such a position didn't currently exist, but if she worked with Julie in the loan department, perhaps she could justify it. A little window of light opened that lent her hope where none had existed beforehand. "Suppose we cared more for what was best for our customers in the long run and made our money the old-fashioned way through interest? Instead, we perch nearby like a pack of foreclosing vultures at the first sign of struggle."

"That would be flock of vultures." He pulled his hat lower over his eyes. When she slapped at his arm, he went on the defensive and broke into a trot. "And I do believe you truly want to take care of your customers, one guy in particular."

She ran after him on impulse to shut his bragging down by catching him.

"Last one to the corner post has to come clean with the truth about their feelings." He posed the challenge over his shoulder and lengthened his stride.

"You're on, long-legged cowboy." She geared up her speed. Breathing would have come easier if she hadn't been laughing so much. The wildflowers went by in a blur as the rock corner post ratcheted ever closer. Soon, all she could think about was the man running in front of her and the way she had begun to feel about him. As the barbed wire finish line approached, she made a final desperate attempt to pass him, but fell short.

He turned and walked the last few steps, resting his hand against the post to claim his prize. She bent and tried to catch her breath, laughing as he made some conciliatory clicking noise at her expense.

"Looks like I'm the winner and you're the confessor." He seemed pleased with the outcome.

She fluffed up her daisy, squished from the exciting sprint, and placed it over one eye. "Okay,

okay." She drew a deep breath before she regarded him. "You have my mind messed up, River Rancher." Her mouth twitched as though it was an unfortunate happenstance. "And my internal compass is messed up with your magnetism. And my organized urban schedule is messed up with my weekend in the country. And my happy-go-lucky existence is now messed up with a pack of goat dependents."

"Herd of goats, you mean." He struggled to keep a straight face. "It seems like I messed up a passel of things for you, Miss City Girl. Was there anything in particular I didn't manage to mess up too badly?"

She stepped closer and scrutinized his face, where his lean jaw line and rugged good looks seared her heart like a direct hit from the sun. She took the daisy and tickled his bottom lip with it, and then found herself trapped in his arms. When he dipped under her hat brim, she tiptoed up to meet him for a merger he got just about perfect, daisies or no daisies. Once the kiss ended, he pulled her back with him against the rock corner post to touch the finish line and it shifted under their combined weight.

"What just happened? An earthquake?" Her tease landed flat in the grass.

Wray's face went through a range of emotions as he processed the sensation. After he glanced over his shoulder, he made an impatient noise that sounded like swearing.

Her concern magnified with every second of his distraction. "What is it, Wray?"

"Someone's dug up this corner post, likely those surveyors who left their card in the door last night. Would those be your Mr. Odom's henchmen, by any chance?"

"No. It's way too early for that, Wray. You'd have to be in your last week or so." Goosebumps raked over her shoulder blade and rushed down her right arm. Maybe something wasn't right here, but she needed to know more. "What else did this card say?"

He worked the post back and forth and it flexed six or so inches. A dirt pile outside the fence lent credence to the tampering claim. "Yesterday's date had been written on the back."

Lacey realized that didn't help much, except to pinpoint the incongruity with their normal default schedule.

"And three letters, R-E-O or something like that."

Goosebumps crossed the valley of her spine and leaked over her left side, trailing down her arm. That linked Mr. Odom's other department, the one that made the aggressive profit for the bank. Her mouth went dry as she tried to form the words. "Wray, I think I might smell a skunk." She rested her hand on his taut shoulder blade.

He shook his head though he couldn't seem to shake off the altered corner post. "Skunks are nocturnal. You wouldn't likely smell one in broad daylight." His tone seemed deflated.

Lacey pulled at his shoulder and made him face her as she noticed the sun wrinkles deepen at the corner of his eyes. His gaze had turned to stone worry. "No. I'm talking about the two-legged kind.REO stands for the Real Estate Owned unit at the bank." A shrill whistle sounded in her mind and she steeled herself at the thought of something inappropriate at the bank. "Wray, I'm going to need that surveyor's card if I'm going to check into this. Julie would believe me without evidence but this might have to go even higher in the ranks. Could you trust me with it?"

His eyes searched hers. "I trust you—but I don't envy your position. Being smack dab in the middle of this is liable to rub you from both directions. Are you sure I'm worth the trouble?"

She closed the gap between them and placed her hand on his chest. That it caught fire resting there had nothing to do with the race to the corner post or the roasting June sun. At least the fire held a vivid sensation, not the mind-numbing effect the rest of her existence yielded.

"You're not the trouble, Wray. They are." Her hand slipped up his shirt and her fingers pulled at the tips of his collar, then traced the placard buttoned across his heart. Perhaps the touch-fire had melted her better discernment, but it felt more like heat forging two individuals into a common destiny. "But there will have to be trust between us, I mean absolute trust whether anyone else can see it or not. Otherwise, delving into this rat's nest won't be worth it for either one of us."

"Absolute trust it is, then." He slipped his arm around her waist.

She could have resisted if she had wanted to, but it was the furthest thing from her intention. Instead, her fire fingers caressed bare skin at the base of his throat.

Wray leaned down toward her. "Father in heaven, this might prove to be a hard thing, as justice often goes. Make the effort be worthwhile without costing Lacey our friendship. Your word promises that nothing kept in secret will escape being made known, so help us bring to light anything that might not be serving innocent people like it should. And I pray you would protect Lacey more than me, as she's the one walking into the lion's den with this, Lord. In the power of Jesus I pray…"

"Don't say 'amen.' Let's live it, Wray." Her insistence came with hushed nuance. Her fingertips brushed his chin scar as he moved toward her and bestowed the benediction she'd hoped for, tender without the hint of pending trouble. They stood together at the wobbly corner post locked in the embrace's duration, a meadow full of wildflowers consenting in the breeze like a host of witnesses all around them.

Chapter 11

Lacey set her hip against her work associate's desk waiting for her weekend dating report to wrap up. Good thing she wasn't as public with the flow of personal information, or neither of them would get any work done.

Julie moved the contents of her in basket front-and-center to address. "Anyway, don't rent the paddle boats right after you've worked your way down the food court at Riverfest. Gerald looked as green as a man can get. And believe me, the color didn't look good on him."

"Julie, can you hold up a minute on those loan tasks?" Lacey wrung her hands and tried not to look desperate. After a long moment, the smirk left her friend's face and a questioning glance took its place. "I have a situation, both personal and bank-related. It's an oddball place to be, so I need you to hear me out."

"Does this have something to do with the tall, dark, and handsome river man that's been on your mind since the first of the month?"

"Halfway." Lacey downplayed the delight that tried to bubble up. "And the other fifty percent has to do with the possibility of something rotten in our REO department."

Julie's plucked brows went airborne and her gaze clouded at the hint of allegation. "Do we need confidentiality?" Her lips barely moved.

"I think we might," Lacey replied.

The flounce of Julie's suit skirt soon led the way into the adjoining conference room. Holding the doorknob, Julie flashed a terse smile at the administrative assistant as Lacey filed past. She motioned toward a seat along the middle of the table and took the chair right beside it. "Tell me everything, straight up and unbiased. If that means you have to tell me both sides of the story from the foreclosing entity and the subject of the foreclosure, so be it. Now let's have it."

"Wray's NOD countdown started June first, Julie. I know because I delivered it myself."

"Oh, I can corroborate that date, as you haven't been the same since."

"Yes, I admit that. I'm not trying to hide anything about my personal involvement there at River Ranch. He invited me out this past weekend."

"Ah, yes. The daisy bouquet. Go on, I'm right with you."

"The fundraiser in Yoder Saturday lasted until nightfall, so we got back to Maize rather late. While we were gone, there was some activity at the ranch which I'll explain in a minute."

The woman's eyes widened but her gaze never

faltered. She nodded for more information.

Lacey received her go-ahead as reinforcement to include as many details as would lend credence to the discovery. "Julie, I want to be real and not cover up how things came about, so you need to know that I stayed at the ranch that night, up in the hayloft in his sister's old hangout. I had slept there Friday night after we finished the prep work on a portable enclosure for the livestock, so I felt comfortable being up there again."

"Although I can think of fifty million girl questions I'd like to ask, let's keep with the storyline on the bank's involvement for now. I do reserve the right to take you out to lunch and find out more about this hayloft arrangement, though."

"On Sunday we attended his church together and spent the afternoon walking the perimeter of his ranch. He wanted me to see the place and every step of it was beautiful, until we got to the far western corner post where trouble began to rear its ugly head."

"Be as specific as you possibly can, Lacey," Julie warned. "We only have one chance to get this right. Any jump to conclusions would discredit your testimony, as most executives would consider you too close to the client already to maintain your professional integrity."

"Okay, here it is. When Wray stopped at the stone fence post, he drew me up to him as he leaned against it and the post moved."

"Was this before, after, or during the kiss?"

"Right after. Good detective work, Julie. You can leave out that part when you relay the story, okay? Anyway, Wray got visibly upset since that post had been in there for generations at the Benson farm. He blamed the trespass on the surveyors who had been out on the property while we were in Yoder."

"How did he know they were on his property? A man can't be two places at once."

"Well, Saturday night when we opened up the house to get a breeze through, a business card slipped out of the front door. We were heading out to the porch swing because Wray was dead on his feet from the livestock auction. I guess he didn't want to spoil the mood so he didn't tell me about the card until the corner post incident."

"The two may or may not be related. Besides, I don't see anything tying either incident to this bank."

Lacey grimaced and produced the business card from her pants pocket.

Julie took it between two fingers and lowered her glasses into place to read the fine type. "'Williams Surveying, the accuracy you want—the service you need.' Okay, the surveyor must have been on the property. Leaving a card in the door is common courtesy in the industry. What does this supposedly tell us as the lending institute?"

"Not as much as the back of the card tells us."

The loan supervisor's brow arched again as her red-tipped fingers twisted the card and held it for closer inspection. A tendon flexed in her slender neck.

Lacey knew the whole case now rested on Julie's professional judgment. A clock on the conference room wall ticked and her pulse raced as the decision to move forward weighed in the balance.

"You sure know how to knot up a Monday, don't you Miss Woodhouse?" Julie's lips slipped into a frown with the understatement.

Lacey held her ground. "If only that knot was already around the skunk's neck. Then we wouldn't have to go traipsing after him."

"And we could avoid the big stink."

Lacey held her breath as long as possible as her confidante worked through the issue.

"Let me state the obvious, so we both understand the gravity of this situation. No one in the first month of their foreclosure should have a surveyor trespassing on their property at the bank's insistence. That is not how Fidelis does business. We respect that three-month window as a final grace period for the loan holder."

"Respect maybe, but we don't offer any advocacy for the family struggling," Lacey replied, her tone knife-sharp.

Julie pursed her lips but took the blow as she flipped the card back and forth in her fingers. "There's no way REO should be working on this yet. You know it and I know it, but what we do about it is not up to us, right now anyway. Girlfriend, you're forcing me to cash in a chip with Mr. Alderman, but I'm going to have to storm into his office and beg his attention, as this has the potential to be a monumental problem for the bank."

"Do what you have to do, Julie. That's why I'm bringing it to you, because I trust you and, quite frankly, I work beside these REO guys nine to five."

"Too close. You're too close on all sides. Give me a day to move on this and then let me come to you. We'll use a code word, something they won't suspect if they happen to overhear it."

A smile quirked the corner of Lacey's mouth. "How about we use 'Gerald?'"

Julie mellowed at the mention of her favorite topic. "That's absolutely luscious. Operation Gerald is hereby underway. May only the good men be left standing in the end."

"Amen, sister. Now I have to go back there and act like nothing's happening."

"You're a good actress, otherwise you couldn't deliver those NODs in the first place."

"Thanks, Julie, for seeing my heart and believing me. It means a lot to me."

"You're part of what's right about this place, Lacey. Don't forget that for a minute."

She rose to exit. "I'll try to remember that when I go out for my next default notification."

Julie stood beside her, gazing as though to size her up. "No one said it couldn't be done with professional sincerity, even if it seems like you're being an agent for the devil himself. Think of it as the start of their redemption period, not the onset of foreclosure."

"Read the bank's REO recovery rate and get back to me on that eventuality," Lacey sniped as she headed for the door.

"I'll come for you tomorrow," Julie promised. "In the meantime, I have at least three more foreclosures headed for your department. We'll process these like nothing's any different than last week."

"Only *I'm* different, and I refuse to go back." Lacey dropped her gaze to her high heels and had to resist the urge to kick them off so she could run free.

~

Wray worked the goat lean-to and finally had the wheelbarrow filled with acrid hay straw. He thought this enclosure would be vacant by now and had to let a smile wander across his otherwise grim countenance as he reflected on how Lacey had refused to let the critters go for a bid less than what they were worth. The kid scampered under the handles and he bent to scratch its bony forehead. Little by little, she saved the ranch by rescuing the rancher from desolation and a solitary existence, at least on the weekends. Being only Monday, the week looked long in the tooth unless he came up with a reason to ask her back out.

He fished his pocketknife out and cut the twine on the new bale of hay straw, scattering it around beneath the feeder trough. The kid tried to come under the lean-to but he tossed a pad of hay to block its path, so it careened in the opposite direction. Maybe Lacey should do the same, turn and run in the other direction, as every entanglement with him at River Ranch spelled trouble for her at the bank. That couldn't feel good to her. He mulled over the conflict of interest with genuine concern. He had prayed about it earlier that morning while he tamped the corner post back into place. It hadn't seemed to help any in the short-term, although he knew it was the right thing to do.

Hank appeared under the gate and came to him inside the shelter. Wray paused long enough to give his herding partner a hearty pat on the flank as the dog tracked an invisible prey across the ground and headed back out. The kid goat scampered away from the dog and ran into the wheelbarrow, bouncing off with a loud bleat.

"Don't get dinged up while your guardian angel isn't here to protect you." He headed for the hay load. "She'd skin me alive if your pretty coat is marked up when she comes back. If only she'd come back." He lifted the handles and shoved the front wheel forward. "Here I go getting soft when what I truly need is to be vigilant." The dog came along and accompanied him to the composting site. With a yank, he pitched most of the hay out of the tub and worked it back and forth until the matted hay cleared.

"Let's get these goats fed and move on to something more enjoyable," he said. The dog gave a bark and pounced with a playful leap as Wray shoved the wheelbarrow back toward the barn. His gaze wandered toward the hayloft and his thoughts drifted to a star-filled night where he learned how to pray and then live it continually by not pronouncing the benediction. "Honey, please don't say the amen," he pled to the vacant barn. A trace of her kiss lingered on his lips. He stowed the wheelbarrow on the far wall and exited to fill the feed trough so he could be done with the goats.

He flipped open the feed room door and squinted into the low light to pull out the goat feed, only to find the bag borderline empty. Under normal conditions, he'd have remembered that and rectified the situation while he was in town running errands. Now, his memory couldn't be trusted as far as his arm could reach. He had too much on his mind and far too much trouble on the horizon to remember something as rudimentary as goat feed. Besides, these animals should have been gone. If Lacey hadn't redeemed them from certain relocation, another farmer would be feeding them today.

Something about his thought progression merged with his underlying desire to get her back out there and worked itself into a credible plan for reuniting them by midweek. At best, he could split what feed remained into two days, especially if he supplemented with some hay. If she could stop by the feed store after work Wednesday, he'd treat her to a cookout and maybe take her horseback riding.

The plan locked itself into his mind as he paced the distance back to the farmhouse. His plan would only be workable if her number was in the phonebook, as he had never thought to ask for it and she hadn't offered. It struck him that his dating skills weren't merely dusty from disuse, they were non-existent.

Hank whined as he kicked through the sunroom door and headed for the kitchen drawers. He snatched the newest phonebook out and flipped toward the back. His finger traced the lettering as it skipped through the W-O section until he found 'Woodhouse' three-quarters of the way down the page. An entry labeled 'L.E.' gave an apartment number for the address, which seemed like his only logical option. He scratched the number down on the notepad and, after a hesitant second thought, the address beneath it and then packed the phonebook back into the drawer. He tore off the sheet and placed the slip of paper by the phone. Too bad quitting time remained half dozen hours away, as his fingers itched to dial her up right then and there.

"Maybe I should clean off the grill to put myself in the best light." He head back out the door. The dog barked and darted back and forth as he made strides toward the garage. "I'm all yours, Hank, until Wednesday evening." Then he willed himself to believe it with all his heart.

Chapter 12

Lacey's key went into the apartment door lock with a grating sound that echoed her feelings for being here. Something akin to an overripe onion assaulted her nose as the door opened and she stepped into a very lonely apartment. Apart from the messy craft corner in the dining area, the place seemed fairly neat, but it struck her as barely livable nonetheless. Only the badly wilted daisy bouquet gave her any positive feedback as she glanced around her living quarters. Funny, she had liked her apartment last week.

She threw off her purse and dropped her keys on the desk. Next, she tied up the reprehensible trash bag to strangle the offensive odor. She loaded up with ginger-soy soap at the sink and remembered how the matching lotion had set Wray's senses on high alert. A pang of loneliness shifted through her as she thought of her solitary week. Her landline rang and she clutched the tea towel to dry her hands.

"Hello?" She cradled the phone on her shoulder to

replace the towel.

"Is this the new owner of five robust goats?"

She allowed the sound of Wray's voice to filter over her and wash her clean of the bank's taint. "Why yes, it certainly is. Have they been a problem for you today, Mr. Benson?"

"Oh, no ma'am. Today they have a freshly cleaned lean-to and a feed trough half full of food and hay. The kid had a minor collision with the wheelbarrow but I talked him through his recovery. I don't believe there will be any lasting scars."

She suppressed a smile and walked the phone over to her stained glass workshop to eye a sketch she'd made of the meadow. "Well, what a relief. I only want the best care for my—herd—as you call it. Nothing but the best for my livestock, after all."

"That's why I called really, as we're going to find ourselves out of goat feed after tomorrow. I wondered if you'd be so kind as to pick some up after work on Wednesday and bring it out. Hank and I would make it worth your while. We could stake out the goats under the orchard and fire up the grill for dinner."

She kicked off her high heels and allowed her heart to react to his invitation without trying to tether it with restraint. "Ooh, that sounds delightful, River Rancher. Are you wooing me or something?"

"I reckon I am, and not so shamelessly either. The weekends seem a far piece apart from each other when you're not out here in between."

"Well, I might have found myself thinking the same thing a couple of times today." She overheard his throaty response and cherished it. "What does a goat food store look like and where would I find one?"

"Go to the feed and seed mercantile on Maize Road. Ask for goat feed in a fifty pound sack and they'll have some young buck load it for you."

She wrote the store name on her wipe-off board on the fridge door. "Consider it done, but I won't be able to get out there much before six-thirty. I hope that's not too late for Hank."

"I'll hold him off with some dog biscuits until you get here, but we'll be glad for the company, I assure you."

"Thank you most kindly, Mr. Benson. I think I rather like this boarding arrangement of my goats at your place. It has hominess to it, so much better than this urban apartment with its steel appliances and total lack of character."

"Oh, we have tons of character out here, more character than grasshoppers, if you can believe that."

"You can keep your bugs. All I want is the wildflowers."

"Is that right? That's all you want, Miss Woodhouse?"

"I can't divulge all my secrets, River Rancher. A lady has to maintain her mystique, after all." When the other end of the line grew quiet for a few seconds, she felt the shift in tone. "I did have my confidential meeting today, by the way. All I can assure you is that the ball is in the official bank court. I'm to wait for my instructions tomorrow. Let me give you an update Wednesday when we see each other face-to-face."

"Does that mean I can't call you tomorrow?"

She drifted back in front of her meadow sketch and wondered how much change came to the landscape in a twenty-four hour period, possibly more than she cared to admit. "Please do call back, as I welcome my daily goat update and any other rural news that might accompany it."

"What a relief." His voice turned velvet over the phone line. "I should give you today's rundown. Let's start with the re-tamping of the corner post this morning right after breakfast."

"Fire away, Farmer Benson, as anything you're doing is of interest to me."

He laughed in the background. "Have you taken your high heels off yet? I can't give the farm report with those intact."

She laughed and spotted the shoes abandoned on the kitchen floor. "Those babies are long gone, as the transition to normal human being only takes a millisecond once I enter the front door."

"Like a real country girl."

A glow filled her with warmth that didn't subside until long after his call had ended. Wray proved good company even over the phone, in part because of his sincerity and in part because she only had to close her eyes to see him in her mind's eye, with stubble on his chin and blue eyes that smiled beneath the brim of his cowboy hat. As her bare feet padded down the hall toward her bedroom, she passed the coat rack. With a flip, she borrowed the pink cowgirl hat, popped it on her head, and began to hum one of the praise songs they'd sung in church together Sunday.

~

Wray watched the midmorning sun play across the river's surface as he rolled into Yoder for a visit. He'd stop at Wren's first, before he delivered the chickens out to Luke's place. The truck slowed and Hank raised his head from the floorboard as though waiting for a command. When the turn for Wren's street came up, he had to decide to break routine and not stop for the cinnamon rolls. No need to keep that illusion going, since he had something real now instead. Sweets didn't seem good to him anyway, as he had family on his mind.

He pulled up to the dirt-lined road in front of his sister's house, fingered the ignition off, and let the truck roll into place. Wren sat out on the porch, her face leaden with the weight of caring for her daughter. Whatever the situation this morning, it didn't look good. He punched the door open and prayed for something meaningful to say.

"God's working on a beautiful day up your way." He stepped up the front stoop. When Wren turned toward him, he could see fresh tear tracks down her cheeks. She wiped them away with the back of her hand as Josh popped out of the screen door and leapt into his arms for his usual hug. "What do you say there, sport?" He rumpled the boy's hair. "I think it was special the way your helped your ma with the chicken noodle dinner on Saturday. That was mighty kind of you."

"I guess. Mr. Luke says I can do anything I put my mind to." The boy squirmed to get down. "Even hard things—like that crazy canopy."

"Run along and play for a minute, will you Joshua? I need to talk to Uncle Wray for a few minutes."

The boy dragged his feet down the steps and headed up the street.

"I'm afraid any beauty God intends for this day is going to be flat wasted on me, Wray."

"Something's got you down, so out with it." He

propped his boot against the whitewashed railing. A red-winged blackbird drank from a puddle on the roadside, sang a series of notes, and then took wing into a small redbud tree across the street.

"She's worse this morning—so much worse she can't lift her head or turn over. Our next doctor visit isn't until two weeks from now. I'm not sure they'll see her early." She paused to draw a breath, and her shoulders shuddered against the chair back.

He could see her fortitude had begun to crumble. "Let me call the doctor and see what I can do. You shouldn't leave her, anyway. Will the meat market let me pay to use their phone?"

She nodded and rocked forward in the chair. "I don't know what more I can do, I really don't. There's so little left of her—and even less of my heart—to withstand what's coming."

"Don't talk like that, Wren. You can pray, pray with all your might for God to hear and intervene. I haven't given up, and you can't either. Let's see what the doctor says. He may have something left to try, we don't know." He wrapped his arm around her shoulders as she stepped to the screen door. Pulling it open with his free hand, he led her into the living room.

Her tear-filled gray eyes stared up into his. "We have the twenty-two hundred and not a penny more. Next month you're set to redeem River Ranch, so your money is no good for any more doctor bills. Do you hear me, Wray?"

A lump formed in his throat as he attempted to corral his feelings into words. When he found the right thing to say, he couldn't even recognize his own voice. "Don't make me look back ten years from now and question if there was anything else I could have done for her. I can't live with that. In the long run, the money won't matter—but having her here with us will."

"If God wants to take her to be with her pa, we can't stop him. I'm fighting the good fight here, but it looks like I'm losing her. There's only so much I can do."

"Let's see what the doctor says. I'll go find out and then drop these chickens off at Luke's place, in case we can get her in today. Maybe you could fix her a bite to eat."

"Take Joshua with you, Wray. I need a break, a quiet break."

"Fine, I know Luke will be happy to see him, anyway."

"Yes, Luke has a grateful heart toward us, you can count on that."

He stepped back out into the sunlight of the day he thought held so much beauty ten minutes ago. *What a difference hope makes.* He returned flat-footed to his truck.

Wren soon came down the steps and handed him a slip of paper with the doctor's phone number on it. She tried to smile but could only pull off a slight flinch.

"Pray—even if you don't know how. Let the Holy Spirit take it from there." When she turned back toward her duty, he eased the truck down the street to pick up the small boy chasing the red-winged blackbird from the picket fence. "Please don't let this happen, God. Remember all your children, especially the ones who can't laugh and play." The bird flew away and left an empty-handed young boy in the middle of the road with nowhere meaningful to go.

Chapter 13

Thick walnut paneling covered the walls of the executive banker's office, which didn't intimidate Lacey one iota as Julie led her in to meet with Mr. Alderman, the bank president. The lean, sharp-featured man stood behind his desk with the phone at his fingertips. Julie settled her into one of two black leather guest chairs and perched halfway in the other. Lacey centered her shoulders toward the executive desk that seemed to demand attention as it weighed one side of the room with authority.

"Hold my calls for the next ten minutes." He disconnected before any reply came and looked up at them with stoic regard. "Miss Woodhouse, I want to thank you for stepping forward with what must have seemed a difficult choice, but the higher road nonetheless."

Though Julie remained expressionless, Lacey gave a slight nod. "You're welcome, Mr. Alderman. Fidelis Bank has given me an excellent start in my professional career, so anything I can do to safeguard it while not compromising my personal integrity is not too much to ask."

He crossed his arms on the desktop and gave Julie a quick glance. "So glad you feel that way, Miss Woodhouse. Now nothing more said in this room today may be discussed beyond the three of us, is that clear?"

"As long as we're on the side of what's legal, it's clear to me," she replied.

He glanced back at Julie whose demeanor melted into a knowing smile and he nodded at her. "Great. That was your first test, and you passed with flying colors, as Julie promised you would. Now, we have to address the issue at hand—our foreclosure department, most specifically, the REO team, and their joint supervisor, Harold Odom."

Lacey's skin crept up her shoulder blades at the inclusion of her immediate boss and she grew uncomfortable. Wray's face flashed in her mind's eye and she forced the unease away. Someone always had to take the heat for the victims in instances like this, and she'd been destined for the role this time. She crossed her ankles and made eye contact with Julie and then the bank president. "I, for one, am ready to know what we're up against."

Mr. Alderman picked up a typed page and held it at reading distance. "Very well, then. Let me give you some background to substantiate the rest. Our success rate with mortgage foreclosures passed the ninetieth percentile last month. That's nearly twenty percentage points higher than the state average, which under any accounting system would be deemed statistically significant. Actually, it would be considered over the top and maybe unheard of in the banking business. Two weeks ago I received a call from the state warning us that we stand to be audited because of this anomaly unless we perform our own investigation and substantiate the rate."

"That's where I came in," Julie said. "Since we start the mortgage process here in our loan department, Mr. Alderman thought he could confide in me. I appreciate that, John."

"You've proven trustworthy time and time again, Julie, so it was instinctive for me to turn to you. But we needed someone in the foreclosure department to serve as our insider for this investigation, and it looks like a hand higher than mine has chosen you, Miss Woodhouse. I might add that I believe strongly that such happenstances have divine guidance and are not to be taken lightly. That sensitivity has served me well over the years and I'm not about to fall deaf to it now, I assure you both."

"I appreciate that, Mr. Alderman," Lacey replied. "God has a hold on me and I feel the changes that accompany his presence."

"Good for you. Now as to our plan, we have to find out what level of impropriety might be transpiring under our bank's sterling name—like this surveyor's business card arriving two months early on the redemption time clock. We have to ferret out each impropriety, document the succession, and build our case. This may run the length of several default cycles, but since you're most closely affiliated with the River Ranch case, we plan to start with it."

Lacey exhaled as new vulnerability shook her at the mention of River Ranch. Wray would volunteer to help. She knew him well enough to anticipate his support.

"Two things have to happen to set this investigation into proper motion," Mr. Alderman said. "First, we have to get you integrated into more of what REO conducts, which I propose in the form of a promotion for you, effective Monday. Secondly, to provide us the legal bearing we'll need to prosecute, I'll have to ask you to curtail your personal involvement at River Ranch at that time."

Lacey's heart thumped against a hollow core at being forced to leave Wray.

"Only for the duration of his redemption period," Julie added. "The irony is—you'll be doing this for him—but he can't know a thing about it. You can let absence make the heart grow fonder in the interim."

Somehow her objection became muted while still in her throat. This was her lot, and it had fallen on an incredibly hard place—her soft spot for the resident rancher.

Mr. Alderman leaned over the desk. "Are you in agreement, Miss Woodhouse?"

She started to balk but Julie held up the surveyor's card as though to say the problem wouldn't simply go away. Mr. Odom's smug face came to mind. The deceit had to stop somewhere, and that somewhere would be River Ranch. "You have my agreement to do this," Lacey managed, "though I don't know how in the world I'll pull it off." As consolation, at least she had until Monday, like an expiring daisy.

~

Wray opened the matching set of doors on the narrow end of the barn and let the midweek sunlight filter into its interior. He hated like anything to start this process, but there didn't seem to be any other way out. With Pleasance's health faltering, the doctor had only one recommendation—an experimental cocktail of cancer-fighting drugs that came with a hefty price tag. Mentally, that money had been earmarked as the redemption payment for the ranch, but now he needed it for this last-ditch effort to save his niece.

Six months ago when he'd started diverting the mortgage payments for her chemo, he never could have dreamed it would have taken so many resources. He'd been an optimistic underwriter without a backup plan, and now it seemed he was in too deep. Without question, he'd cover the cost of treatment, down to his last cent if he had to. But the price would be steep, and River Ranch might teeter on the brink of forfeiture in the fallout.

He scanned the walls of the barn and made an inventory of all the gear and tack that hung from hooks and pegs around the stalls. This barn served as a museum of Benson effort, which started with his grandfather's first day of farming and extended through today. That heritage of leather harnesses, worn hand tools, and abandoned steel plows was of considerable importance to him, but would be mere junk to the next potential owner. Perspective became everything— perspective coupled with possession, which slipped from his hand with every crosshatch drawn on the kitchen calendar.

His boots stirred the dust as he walked into the barn's interior. He needed a large storage unit where he could stash the usable items and then pitch the rest. He opened the pedestrian door to get additional light and caught sight of the livestock trailer. Its roomy insides and portability lent the capability he needed. In two shakes of a goat's tail, he strode out the door toward his truck to make the hook-up. Hank followed along behind him past the large elm.

"She'll be here this evening, old boy. But should we tell her? In the end, we'll fold our hand so the bank wins, right?" The truth stung the back of his throat. He tried not to mix his feelings for her with the bank's inevitable victory, but in his sad state it all became muddled together like a tangled ball of twine.

"Kennel, Hank." He opened the truck door to get the cleanout underway. *It's only a short trip for us.* The redemption period had been carved down to ten weeks already. Lacey's face came superimposed over the image of a calendar page, her green eyes fiery with indignation at his inept financial management. He revved the engine, threw the truck into reverse, and backed out of the empty garage that epitomized his life.

~

The sweet smell of molasses hung in the air as Lacey wandered into the feed store, anxious to get the order right but unfamiliar with the process. Some sparkly cowgirl trimmings shined up the front counter area where she stepped up to ask for assistance. No one seemed to be working there. She looked up and down several aisles and then made her way toward a muffled sound coming from the back storage area. Two men emerged and worked a saddle stand into place on the display floor behind the register. The older man straightened out with a hand on his hip and made a low moan.

Lacey stepped into view. "Hello there. I was

hoping someone could help me with some goat feed."

The younger man pointed toward the back and followed his own signal while the moaner took the register and began to ring up the sale. "Got some goats out this way, then?" he asked in a husky voice. "Haven't seen you by before today."

She smiled and produced her wallet. "I bought some goats over the weekend and am boarding them at a friend's farm. Will that young man load the feedbag for me? I don't think I can manage fifty pounds."

The total rang up and he looked at her with tired gray eyes. "Sweetheart, I don't think I can manage fifty pounds any more either, so Junior had better load it or we're both in a fix."

She pulled out a credit card and he processed the purchase in methodical slow-hand. The burly helper reappeared with a feed sack over his shoulder and motioned to the door. She hesitated until the cashier handed her the receipt and then jogged to catch up to the deliveryman. Popping the trunk remotely, she cued him toward her car and soon realized how small her storage capabilities were. When the sack hit bottom, the car's rear shocks complained.

Junior tipped his ball cap back with a grin. "Are you going to be able to get that out?"

"I've got Wray on duty at the other end."

"Wray Benson? He's a buddy of mine. Tell him we're still friendly around here—even if he's got his credit maxed out right now. No need to be a stranger on account of money."

Lacey felt the financial sting as Wray's proxy. "You say his store account is to the limit?"

"That's what Dad tells me, but you know it doesn't

matter to me. If a man needs to feed his animals, he ought to be able to somehow."

Determined to be an agent of assistance, she had to set matters straight. "Let's go back inside to settle this account. I'd like to take care of that outstanding balance today if I could. That way he can feel free to come around the next time he needs something."

"That's mighty nice of you."

"Lacey. I'm Lacey Woodhouse, a new friend of Wray's." The admission had a cleansing effect, which washed over her as they reentered the mercantile. This time the molasses smell proved even sweeter. The younger man retrieved a ledger book from under the register and flipped through several pages while the older proprietor fiddled with the stirrups dangling from the display saddle.

"Maybe somebody in high times would like something as fine as this," the old man mumbled, his back to the register.

"Possibly." Lacey grew anxious to hear the credit total. She could afford to cushion his debt by taking care of this loose end. Besides, Wray needed to concentrate his efforts on pulling out of the default on his mortgage. Once that was underway, he'd have time to breathe a little and address other outstanding issues—and maybe even spend time with his reinstated girlfriend.

"Three hundred and fifty dollars—if you aim to pay the whole tab." Junior double-checked the amount. The old man straightened, now clued to what was transpiring, and shuffled his boots to reexamine the ledger.

"Sure, let's clear the whole credit line and get him

back in good standing," Lacey replied. She started to produce her credit card but the elder clerk shook his head at that method of payment. She reached for a pen on the counter and flipped her checkbook open. "Let's get this settled once and for all. I could even prepay for another bag of feed if you'd let me."

"No, ma'am. No paying ahead of time. We don't operate like that. I've been doing business with the Benson family for over forty-five years. There's no dishonor between us. Wray's had a bad go of things, losing his folks like he did. We all wish him the best."

She tore the check out and offered it to the younger man and he rang it into the register. "You know, his niece has been sick with leukemia. Once she turns around, he'll be back on top of things. His wheat looks promising and he just sold off his herd to have more cash flow."

"Well, tell him we hope the little girl gets better in no time," the old man replied. "Most days none of us are sitting high in the saddle—just ordinary days with ordinary folks."

She watched as the ledger was marked "paid in full." Maybe Wray would like to know. "Can you make out a receipt and then mail it out to the Benson place for me?"

"Be glad to, ma'am. And let me add that things seem to be looking up for Wray already." The old man winked to punctuate his meaning.

A flush started up her neck and she stepped toward the exit as fast as she could.

"Come back and see us anytime."

She tossed a wave as daylight saved her from her own embarrassment. Now she had approximately nine miles of washboard country roads to shake the blush from her neck before meeting Wray. If she thought about him the whole way out, the blush would only deepen. It might be a better time to think about her predicament at the bank. That should be situation enough to squelch any true emotional response her hormones could muster.

~

Wray set the plate of hamburger patties into the refrigerator when he heard her tires on the gravel out front. Still wet from his hurried shower, his hair disappeared under his Sunday hat as he strode out of the kitchen. With a bang of the screen door, only grass separated the two of them. Well, maybe the full disclosure of the truth counted, which he was reluctant to release. He'd decided not to tell her about Pleasance until the girl had time enough to react to the doctor's new treatment. No need to worry other folks with the ups and downs of her ailment.

Lacey stepped out of her car with her hair loose and flowing in the late afternoon breeze. Her trunk popped open as Hank ran out for a watchdog greeting. She gave the dog a hug.

Wray cocked a smile to one side thinking how the clever canine managed to one-up him at every turn. "Save some of that lovey-dovey stuff for the lonely rancher." Hank barked in sheer joy as her fingertips ruffled the hair along its back.

Lacey laughed. "There's plenty of lovey-dovey to go around, River Rancher. Don't you worry. And would you accept fifty pounds of assurance to make sure my goats stay well-fed?" A humble bleat came from the corral and she started to divert her step toward it.

Wray caught her arm and pulled her to him for a welcome back hug. "Thanks for giving me a new reason to adore Wednesdays," he whispered through her hair.

She giggled into his neck. After scratching circles into his back, she released him, ran toward the corral, and chanted baby talk to the goats. The kid scrambled under the gate and ducked her grab for a mouthful of grass.

Wray spread his feet to lift the feedbag. "See. Not everybody is as huggable as I am." He grunted for emphasis and hoisted the sack onto his shoulder while the dog ran in arcs behind him. "Come get the door for me, will you?"

She hesitated but came jogging along the corral fence to catch up with him. "Where to?"

"Pull on the hook midway up the back wall there." He nodded toward the lean-to.

She scrambled to stay ahead of his pace and find the portal matched into the back wall. Her painted nails pinched the hook and her shoulders forced it to comply, opening the storage room of the structure without a second to spare.

The sack shifted off his shoulder and fell into the feed room like clockwork. He shoved the door closed and set the hook to end their chore list to focus on something more fun.

Her eyes sparkled with excitement. "Can I brush the little darlings?"

"They've never been brushed before," he countered. "What if they don't like it?"

"And what if they do? I want to give it a try.

They're my goats now and I need to take care of them, right? It can't be all fun and games when I come out here." She glanced around the farmyard. "I want to work in the orchard, too. Is there something we can do?"

"I suppose we could trim away the sucker branches to give the fruit more nourishment. I haven't got to prune them yet this summer."

"Perfect—and then we can cook out and have fun. There will be plenty of time for it all. I'll even stay late if I have to. And I want to make sure we pray for Pleasance before I go."

"Oh, definitely. And for Wren, too. Guess you could say the pace has been a bit much for her lately. The good news is she's letting Luke come courting every day. He's got my chickens now—I don't remember if I told you that would happen."

"Good riddance to those squawkers," she replied. "Now where can a girl find a good brush to make a goat look presentable?"

"Wow. Somebody has a favorites list that doesn't include poultry."

She stepped up to him and rested a hand on his forearm. Mischief played around her eyes. "You're right. I do have a favorites list, and it's a short one. I wouldn't buck against someone trying to make this place better by spit-shining the livestock now and then, if I were you."

He laughed and hooked an arm around her waist. Once he hoisted her onto his shoulder like a feed sack, he stepped toward the tack room in the barn where a ledge of brushes and curry combs waited. She pulled at his belt in retaliation but he decided to even enjoy that.

Halfway there, her laughter started trickling out and was highly contagious. When her feet found the hay on the barn floor, she tried to regain her focus. "You don't have to harness and tote me around like some uncooperative female, Wray."

"I'm only showing you where to go, city girl. I'll let you pick your own mode of transportation next time. Now here's the tack room, so come choose your brush." The tack room had been plenty big until he'd cleaned up. Now he had extra leather harnesses stored inside and the space seemed to shrink when he stepped in behind her.

She gave him a satisfied tweak of her mouth. "I think I'll try this one. They wouldn't like the metal comb-thing would they?"

"You can try both and see what works best. With goats, you never know." He smiled and blocked the doorway even though he knew she was ready to get busy.

"Let's get with it then, out we go," she insisted.
He stepped aside but not far enough that they didn't have to bump through the doorway.

She turned sideways and slid through. "Hey, I think I see my chariot waiting, if you're serious about letting me pick."

"Pick away, but that leaves the possession arrow pointing back at me."

"I pick the wheelbarrow, then. I want you to push me out there to the corral like my grandfather used to do in his garden."

He laughed as a similar memory popped into his head and stepped around her for her chariot of choice. "Good thing I gave this a wash-off after its last load, or

I think you'd be changing your mind right about now."

"No sour grapes, Wray. Unfortunately with this particular pick, one of us becomes the lackey. You push first and if you're nice later, I'll push you."

"Now that I've got to see—and I'm picking a loop around the orchard for my trip." She slid into the wheelbarrow when he lowered the front lip of the bucket. Once they were clear of the barn door he escalated to a trot and forsook the straight line back to the corral. Lacey dropped the brush to hang on to both sides but laughed like a carefree little girl the entire way. Eventually, they got to the corral gate where he tipped the bucket forward and graciously allowed her to regain her feet.

"That was extremely awesome. Now what are you going to do?"

"What if I stretch out under the elm to watch you work?"

She lifted her chin and studied the wooden benches under the elm. "What if you clean out the goat's water trough? That way I'll have fresh water to clean up in afterwards."

The memory of how he'd first encountered her draped over the trough side came back to him, her bare legs glistening in the hot June sun. "Reckon that would keep me busy for awhile. Maybe I'll water the garden with the cast-offs. Pardon me while I go fetch my buckets."

She caught the kid goat by the collar and drew him to her for closer inspection. Her nose wrinkled and she glanced up with a rather pathetic look.

"Remember you wanted to do this."

"Oh, I do. I hope the goat smell comes off with

soap and water."

"You mean fresh, cool well water, as no soap is going into my water trough."

She puffed her bangs out of her eyes, settled in beside the kid, and rubbed its forehead with her fingertips.

Wray turned away before any seeds of jealousy could germinate and hastened to retrieve the water buckets. They'd probably smell like goats before the day ended, which served them both right for gravitating toward ornery-cute.

Chapter 14

Grilled beef sent a heavenly aroma across the backyard, and Lacey's stomach growled. Twilight hinted toward a milky shade of aqua behind the crowns of the orchard trees as she snapped a time-creased tablecloth across their makeshift dinner table. Wray appeared with a tray laden with condiments and the bowl of salad she had hastily tossed.

He slid the tray onto the table. "How's your big dry-off coming?"

"Almost there," she replied. When his hand brushed her hip as though to test it, she swatted it away with a giggle. "Remember, we need to save time for your ride around the orchard after dinner."

"Unless I change my mind, which I might." He backtracked toward the house.

She examined the little cottage as daylight dimmed around it and wondered how many meals had been shared there in love and safekeeping. If a ripple in such continuity approached, she didn't feel it one bit. The evening settled in with cozy stillness and she strained to hear the river flow by, but the birdsong from the orchard proved too insistent.

Wray banged out of the screen door with two chrome chairs from the kitchen.

"Can you bring the lantern out? I think we may need it before the meal is done."

"Flip the burgers for me and I'll make the illumination happen." The chairs found opposite sides of the table and he jogged back to the house.

She strolled over to the grill and grabbed the tongs. Before she could get all the patties turned, the mosquitoes seized upon her ankles in full force.

The screen door opened and he stepped to her side in seconds.

She slid her free hand down her bare leg. "Bugs are biting already."

"It's the heat from the grill drawing them in. How about you go get a spare tablecloth and wrap up? Or we could relocate into the sunroom and outfox them."

"I'll try the cover-up option. If we keep the table away from the grill's heat, maybe we can buy some time. I'll be right back out. Do we need anything else?"

"Go ahead and bring the tea out. I don't think we have much longer on these."

"Will do. I like my burgers more medium than well, so don't burn them on my account."

"No burning. Got it." He flashed an appeasing smile over the grill's glow.

She retreated away from the ankle-biters and toward some relief. Returning to the same drawer in the kitchen, she selected a larger tablecloth, fluffed the folds out, and wrapped it around her waist. The worn linen tucked coolness against her skin and provided cover clear down to her ankles. She found the tea pitcher and grabbed two plastic glasses waiting beside it.

On her way out, she paused to glance at the farm calendar hanging by the sunroom steps. Wray had numbered the days of his redemption period and crossed off those days that had already elapsed. She noted the insurance company that had printed the calendar with their motto "Coverage you can count on." She wondered if that could be true, given the state of affairs at River Ranch. Maybe she could check into that policy as part of her research. Wray called out and broke her train of thought, so she headed outside. "Here I am." She lifted the pitcher up like a peace offering.

"Burgers are ready. Not burnt, but medium and juicy, just like the lady ordered."

"Well thank goodness some things can be made-to-order." She came up beside him as he scraped the grill clean. The lantern glowed on his face as he concentrated on his task, so she studied his features in the soft light. God perfected the made-to-order business, as she couldn't imagine a better-looking man to sit across the table from. He turned toward her and she blinked so he couldn't read the admiration in her eyes. She may have been too late, as he bent and gave her a quick kiss right there in mosquito haven.

"Nice cover job." He glanced down her length.

She blushed and her breath caught, until she realized he referred to her tablecloth wardrobe. "Please don't drop the burgers. I'm starving. In fact, I'd race you to the table but I'm tied up tighter than a potato sack."

"Well, squiggle your way over and we'll eat. Or I could throw you over my shoulder again."

"Don't you dare! I'll manage on my own this time. You keep Hank off my skirt-tail and I'll be fine."

He whistled the dog to his side, which wasn't hard since he carried the meat platter. The little table shrank under the delivery and their plates had to squeeze to the edges.

"Are we running out of room?"

"Well, since I was going for cozy, the answer is no."

"Oh, yes. Let's go for one hundred percent cozy," she replied. The lantern light snuffed down a few notches. She settled into her chair and looked up at him. When his gaze fixed on hers, the lock-up proved fairly heady. "Here's a tribute for made-to-order," she posed as she poured tea into both of their glasses.

He took the glass but didn't speak, his blue eyes saying everything.

She reached for him across the table and he met her hand with his. She discovered closing her eyes next to impossible.

Wray bowed his head and uttered a humble prayer but held off on saying amen. Before she could respond, he lifted her hand, kissed her fingers, and released them back to her.

"Thank you for having me out, Wray. This place truly makes me feel at home."

He nodded as he passed her a burger, as though he already knew it.

~

The porch swing squeaked in rhythm, and Wray decided to voice his offer before the night grew too late to see if she'd be willing. After all, life comprised more than work and suffering, which he seemed to lose himself in lately to the exclusion of making merry. With Lacey's appearance, he had an excuse to slow down and smell the daisies.

"I've been thinking about something for us to do this Saturday, if you're available and willing."

She tucked in closer beside him. "Depends on what kind of adventure you have in mind."

"Today while I was starting a cleanup in the barn, I found Dad's old wooden canoe in the rafters. I thought it might be fun to drop it in upriver and see if it still floats."

"Ooh, that sounds like fun. I'd enjoy seeing more of the river. Where would we put in?"

"We could start at the bridge up in Halstead, leave the truck and paddle down to River Ranch, where we'd haul the boat back up from the lower pasture. You could drive me back to Halstead for the truck afterward. That should take us most of the morning while it's nice and quiet out. What do you think?"

"Count me in. I claim the bow. The steering part in the stern always proved a little tricky for me back in summer camp."

When her eyes danced at the thought of adventure, he knew he'd done the right thing. Maybe spending time together would be his new focus, as courting her held the only glimmer of light in his otherwise struggling existence.

"Do we have everything else we need for the float? Paddles? Life vests?"

"Well, I found the paddles up there, but I bet the life jackets were pitched years ago." He shoved off to keep the swing in motion as the night reclaimed its silence.

"I'll ask Julie if I can borrow a couple. Her beau Gerald owns a boat. They go to Cheney Lake every other weekend when the weather's good. And we could toss together a picnic lunch. I can bring the food out Friday night and fix it right before we go."

"Friday night, huh? Sounds to me like somebody might be missing their chic nook up in the hayloft." He dropped his arm around her waist. His chest tightened when she laid her head back and her silky hair covered his T-shirt.

She brought her wrapped legs up and wiggled into a comfortable position. "I might be missing something, but the hayloft is only a small part of it." Her voice drifted soft and low.

He thought she looked like a dream in the dim light filtering through the bay window from inside, so he touched the swing's support chain to prove the moment was real. "I want you out here with me. I hope you know that. And I hope you feel it like I do." He bent toward her delicate face.

Even in the darkness her eyes sparkled, and she gazed back at him, open and unhesitant. "I feel it, God help me, I feel it, Wray. The timing seems so crazy though."

He brushed back her hair. "Crazy against the grain of everything else that's going wrong."

"How about we trust God's plan and allow it to happen despite the circumstances. I wouldn't want to miss out on a blessing he intended for me, and I wouldn't wish that for you either. Life's hard enough not to trust. Don't you agree?"

He leaned back on the slatted swing and contemplated her question. With every day that ticked by, he was losing his farm to the bank and his niece to a voracious disease. God shredded him down to the bone in one moment and brought Lacey to him the next. But what good was a rancher without his ranch—or a family man without his kinfolk? The irony only made his situation more difficult to comprehend. "Lacey, I may hit rock bottom when this all plays out, I have to warn you. I won't let it shake the core of my faith, but I can honestly say that I don't know what God's up to or why I have to go through all this agony-on-top-of-agony. What if I come out a different man on the other side? What if I fail the test? I wouldn't want you to fall for a rancher who might be dispossessed of everything he owns."

"Not everything," she whispered, as she pulled him toward her.

With her eyes like liquid beacons, he couldn't fight the draw even if he'd wanted to. Bent over her, the miracle of it all swept over him and a lump filled his throat.

"Besides, it's a little late if you're hoping I don't fall for you," she replied.

"Praise God I didn't manage to mess that up." His lips moved slow as he surveyed the tender terrain of her face. Emotion pooled in her eyes and he thought he saw the stars again, reflected in their warmth. He could be discovering an uncharted constellation that required navigating in a new direction. When his lips met hers, he gave way to the sensation of being adrift in the vacuum of love and allowed the porch swing vessel to take him away to ports unknown. Time stood still when they were this close, as though in full denial of the advancing erosive tide. The kiss melted into a clutched embrace and they held each other into the night.

~

Lacey gave her lunch partner a few extra seconds to respond to her request.

Julie turned her water glass full circle. "Life jackets for the weekend? Are you insane?"

Lacey held her ground, sure of what she had planned. "It's our last weekend together. I want it to be special. The river is Wray's special place." A waitress came up and delivered a small plate of assorted crackers.

"Sounds like an aquatic train wreck to me," Julie countered. "Maybe you should pull the fickle female routine and cop out early. You know, cut the line and not leave him dangling like some pathetic hooked fish. Sometimes this dating game comes down to who's going to survive, you or him."

Lacey squinted her disapproval as she opened a pack of Captain's Wafers. "We've agreed to trust God to see where the relationship will go." She skimmed the cracker across her lips. The buttery flavor helped soothe her senses.

"You know where it's going, girlfriend," Julie insisted. "It's heading into mothballs for three months, minimum. I don't know how you plan to keep love's flame alive over that period of separation unless, of course, mothballs are volatile."

"I think they are flammable, but our separation isn't the point, Julie. It's what you do with the time you're together that matters. Time apart is an obstacle, but if we're meant to be, God will get us past this hurdle and on with life together."

"If a ranch-less, penniless man can allow himself to love, that is."

"When did you become such a cynic when it comes to men?"

"Oh, about boyfriend number eight or so. One doesn't spend a lifetime being single and not learn a few hard lessons, dearie."

"Guess you never found that Mr. Alderman type who was your perfect match."

Her confidante blushed at the innuendo and fussed over placing her napkin in her lap. "Never found him in time," Julie corrected in an icy tone. "John married while we were still juniors in college. I suppose they couldn't wait. Such is the impetuous nature of love, which is why I try to reason my way through it instead. Being rational makes more sense, and there's a whole lot more control."

"When you walk in faith, you've already surrendered that control, Julie. When I allow God to lead, it gives me the opportunity to be molded to his will, which always aims for my good." The waitress stepped up, balancing two rather large salad bowls with thin slices of chicken gracing the top of one. Lacey paused and let her situate the food to her liking before making her final point. Once the server had stepped away, she leaned across the table and fixed her gaze on her co-worker. "I couldn't walk into the lion's den I'm heading for without that shield of faith. If God is for me, then who can be against me?"

"How about a crooked REO unit?" Julie chirped with indignation.

"Bring it on come Monday, but give me my

weekend on the river first." Lacey selected her fork and made a stab into the heart of the salad mound, ready for whatever came next.

"Okay, I'll ask Gerald for the life jackets so you can have your weekend prelude to heartbreak and isolation. Remember who told you to cut your losses and run while you could, as this has all the makings of a disaster at the deepest level. Now please let me enjoy this salad as a reminder of my perpetual diet."

"Thank you, Julie. Try to bring them in Friday if you can." She delivered the first succulent bite to her lips. Well into the heart of her romaine feast, her lunch partner nodded in consent. Lacey couldn't deny the prick from her friend's REO comment, but she would choose to step into that tainted arena when the time came. First, she had to live a little.

~

Wray admired the layout of Luke's corral as they walked out to his proposed storage site. Before them, an unused grain silo vaulted above the horizon. The wheat field beyond the grounds swayed in the Kansas wind.

"Looks like your wheat might be a day or so ahead of mine."

"Probably, as we're further west than you are," Luke replied. "We wouldn't want the custom cutters to bust a vein trying to get all the wheat cut at once, now would we?"

He caught the wry tease in Luke's voice and gave a chuckle.

"What about you, Wray? You ever thought about hiring out—you know, if you lose your place to the foreclosure?"

Wray shifted his hat and ran his hand across the

back of his neck as he weighed the suggestion. "Reckon I've got the equipment for it, which is what started this crazy down-spiral in the first place."

Luke shot him a quizzical look.

He reached down deep to admit the flawed financial plan. "Dad took out a second mortgage on River Ranch to upgrade the equipment when the old International grain truck went belly-up on him. In hindsight, we could have done that in phases, but he took the lead and I held my peace about it at the time. It's so obvious now that we disregarded common sense with regard to major debt, but we couldn't see the grain elevator tragedy coming."

"Nobody's blaming you, Wray. It's just how things happened."

"Well, I always thought I could make it up down the line. Our farm income always came in steady, especially when beef prices stayed strong and grain prices held. Losing Dad was a gut punch to our productivity and I've been busting my chops ever since he's been gone. Then Pleasance faltered and I couldn't stand by and let that happen."

Luke stopped in front of the grain silo and looked at him, long and hard. "God's in charge of that one, Wray. You've done more than what one man can do. Wren told me about your financial backing of all the medical bills. I blame Josiah's lack of insurance planning for that, but just the same, I wish I could have been there for Wren earlier."

"She probably wasn't ready, Luke, so don't hang that burden on yourself."

"The favor of God's hand is on me now, though. She's such a remarkable woman, despite all the pain and loss. You know I'm honored to keep company with her. I go to town most every day so she can tell me what's on her heart. There's nothing I wouldn't do for that time together."

"Tell me about it. I think Lacey and I are coming to the same place. It does have a saving grace to it." He pulled the lever to open the door, and then peered into the dusty bin. He found nothing inside but wide open space begging for storage of the unnecessary. It would be an undignified interim, but being caught in the in-between didn't have to be fancy.

"Wray, before you pull up and unload, I want to show you my latest project." Luke nodded toward the barn.

He left the silo door open and followed a half step behind his host. With no explanation offered, he let it go as they crossed the barnyard. Rain clouds threatened over the tin roof of the barn, and he realized he had forfeited the ten o'clock news to his late company last night. "Do we have rain in the forecast? Guess I missed the weather report last night." A sheepish grin worked its way over his face, though he tried to downplay it.

Luke cut his gaze away and regarded the storm clouds. He delayed his reply as though he had something simmering on his back burner. "Brother to brother, I hope you're keeping it respectable with your courting Lacey. I know nobody's there to chaperone you two, but sometimes a man's honor is all he's got."

"I appreciate that word of caution from an old friend who might someday be that brother. We've put God first in our friendship so I can brag of a strong start anyway."

"The proof's in how you end." Luke shoved the

barn door open. Daylight suffused the interior as the farmer led a few steps inside. There in a workshop corner sat a small wooden coffin, nearly finished.

Blame it on the wood dust, but Wray could hardly breathe in.

"Some endings are not in our control, but others are."

Wray admitted that he possessed less control than was comfortable, especially for an independent, self-employed rancher. "Mighty thoughtful of you, Luke." He wished with all his heart that the coffin and the grain silo could remain empty.

"Let's get you unloaded so I can get to Wren's before the rain comes." Luke's hand found Wray's shoulder. His gray eyes held a sea of understanding.

"I appreciate a man that can make the hard chore easier." He hung his head at circumstances beyond his control. "Let me give you a ride up to Wren's afterward."

"I'd be much obliged for it," Luke admitted as they fell into step together.

An age-old habit, Wray checked the western sky again and could tell rain would set in before nightfall. At least the wheat would get a drink as it matured and the river level would be up. That could mean a few less portages over sandbars for Lacey on Saturday. Try as he might, he could barely recall her face at the moment, as the little coffin settled on his mind's eye front and center. Maybe the rain would wash that away, too, if he prayed hard enough.

Chapter 15

Lacey spent the workday Friday organizing her desk, unsure what Monday morning would bring. Hopefully, she could carry on with her delivery of NODs, as she now had a new tactic in her arsenal called compassion. At Julie's direction, she had kept the three new default clients in her in-box for processing on Monday under "Operation Gerald." She read back over their names and launched into involuntary prayer right there with her eyes wide open.

"Babbling over them isn't getting the bank any closer to recovering its assets," a nasal voice asserted. She turned to find her supervisor standing right behind her chair.

"The clock starts for these three on Monday, Mr. Odom. Today I'm becoming familiar with the cases."

"Never put off until tomorrow what you can do today, young lady. Mind if I take a look?" He extended a hand, insistent on the payload.

She complied with a lump in her throat, feeling the

pressurized pull between protection and exposure. His proximity made her skin crawl, and she rubbed the back of her neck under the pretense that her hair barrette required attention. Diverting her gaze to her phone console, she noticed that Julie's light switched off that instant. Without thinking it through, she punched her button and lifted the receiver.

"Hi, Julie, I wanted you to know that I reviewed the three case files and will be ready to move on them Monday," she said, her tone professional. She paused to allow the reply and glanced up with a curt smile at the balding man who eavesdropped on their conversation. "I'll make sure they stay on my desk until then. See you Monday morning—and thanks for the loan." She hung up the receiver and pushed the bag of life jackets further under the desk with her foot.

"Thanks for the loan," he repeated in a cloying falsetto. "That's a line I rarely hear." The files plopped back into her in-box with juvenile surrender as he turned and wandered back to the vulture zone with the REO group.

She tried to halt the shudder as it moved up her back but it caught her off guard, flaunted by a coward's head start. She opened an electronic agenda file, typed the word "Gerald" on Monday's space, and counted the days remaining in the month. How many twenty-four-hour periods could "interminable" possess?

~

The canoe leaned against the water trough, gleaming in the late afternoon sun. Wray hung the rag on the lowest branch of the elm tree and examined the vessel for seaworthiness. He hadn't found any gaping holes in its hull but wasn't sure that time had been too kind to the varnished exterior. The intricate work of the caning seats reminded him of his mother's handiwork, and a smile cropped up from nowhere.

"Guess I forgot to ask you if you wanted to go boating down the river," he said to his companion. Hank lifted his head and whined a little, tired from vigilant duty with the kid goat. A red flash interrupted their one-way conversation and he let the surprise ripple through him. She'd arrived early. On automatic attraction, he headed toward her car as it stopped in front of the garage. He pulled the door up and she eased in, paying for her valet treatment with a generous smile.

"Now it's officially the weekend." He bowed like an usher as her car door swung open. Hank lumbered up and added his bark.

The driver looked over her sunglasses at the two of them. "A lady could get used to such an endearing reception." Lacey swung her legs out to stand.

Wray lent her a hand, which she accepted, although the dog prevented him from completing the intended hug. "I'm afraid we're acting like we don't get much company around here."

"Well, the road's a little washboard for drop-by company." She rose on tiptoe to look him full in the face. "City folk don't like washboard. It makes them slow down."

"And you, Miss Woodhouse? Do you want to slow down?" He draped his arm across her shoulder to help direct her response.

"I seem to be enjoying the scenery around here. Nice wildflowers and all. I've heard there's a river, but what a pity no one's shown it to me yet."

"I'm promising you the river tour tomorrow. Right

now I can hardly wait to show you the vintage vessel that will take us afloat. Let's get you unpacked first and then we'll load the canoe on the truck. It's definitely a two-person job."

"Sounds like a plan, but maybe we should make a deal before we get started."

"What kind of deal?"

"How about no mention of anything inside the city limits that would spoil our weekend? Can we do that— at least until I'm about ready to leave Sunday night?"

"Huh, must have been a tough week. You've got it, green eyes. Now conversing only about the countryside."

"Cute stuff like kid goats and baby owls can be included, of course."

"Cute stuff." He drew her toward him, face to face. In a subtle claim, he wrapped his arms around her back and scooped her off the ground. He'd skip the routine unpacking for now, as they had better things to do.

~

The giant elm held the only respite for the late afternoon heat, and Lacey had already dipped into the water trough twice between helping Wray load the canoe onto overhead racks on the truck. Old-timey wood turned out to be old-fashioned heavy, and her arm muscles retained the lasting strain. The goats bleated in staccato while she remained in sight, so she plucked a handful of grass to buy herself a moment of silence. To her relief, a pad of hay soon flew over the fence for protracted appeasement.

"Before night falls, how about we walk them down to the river pasture where my horse stays? I can show you my stretch of river so you'll recognize it when we pull in tomorrow."

"Yes to the goat thing, but you may be giving me too much credit for landmark recognition. Maybe I should use my phone to take a picture."

"Take a picture up here." He tapped her cowgirl hat. "That's all the equipment you need. Focus on something unusual along the bank, and you'll pick up on that when you see it again. That always works for me, anyway." He stepped toward the trough and splashed his neck.

"I think that's how I navigated back out here in the first place." Her mouth tucked into a smirk. Occupied with chores, she hadn't caught him looking at her very often. She tossed her hat onto the bench under the elm and allowed the breeze to cool her forehead. A monarch butterfly skittered by on its way to some flowering bushes on the corner of the house. She ran her fingers across her temples to pull some strays back, when the fabric tie holding her hair gave way. The wind tousled her long black hair as she turned to find him standing there, transfixed on her profile. She melted under his stare. "It's hot like this."

"Tell me about it." His words came slow and husky. He offered her the hair tie that rested blameless in his hand.

She repositioned it, knowing he studied her every move. "Let's eat now, Cowboy. You've worked me into anemia."

"I've got a fix for that. Get your hat and climb up on the bench."

She sensed a game coming on but didn't quite know the venue until he backed up in front of her and gestured to his shoulders. She planted her hands with a girlish laugh and jumped aboard the piggyback express. When he stepped into a loping gallop, she pulled closer, her sweat mingling with his damp shirt in a cooling mix. Their hat brims collided at his every footfall until she lowered her face into the crook of his neck. "This is truly first class." Her lips grazed his skin as she spoke. She soon caught a vista full of the orchard, the corral, and the eternal elm anchoring it in place. "I'm taking one of those mind photos right now, by the way."

She wet her lips and they tasted like him—earthy and salt seasoned. The view stopped when his foot hit the brick back steps, and she found herself being flung around his shoulder in continued momentum. Steadied at her waist, her laughter tailed off when she caught the focused look in his eyes.

"Let me get in the picture," he insisted, "so you'll remember me."

Only one answer existed for that request, so she pulled her hat off and found the next step, putting her level with his intense blue eyes. "Truth be told, I'm having a hard time thinking of anything else." The admission flooded a molten surge up her neck into her cheeks. She longed to close the gap between them when he tucked her to his chest. The ardent kiss filled her senses. Then something unlatched deep inside. She kissed him back and held on for more than support, as she was adrift in this river of love and had no idea where she would land.

~

"Let's see how much cooperation we're gonna get." Wray tightened his grip on triple lead lines. "You've got the carrots, right?"

Lacey struggled to get the kid to even up with its

mother, a notoriously wayward beast. "For what little good it's going to do me. No wonder you haul them around in a trailer." She tugged, and the nanny planted its hind feet, dead set against her.

"Tuck a carrot in your back pocket, then get in her vicinity. You could even let her have the first bite. Then you can play hard to get after she's interested."

"It's worth a try, or I won't see the river tonight." She tore the carrot bag open and several fell to the ground where the dutiful kid cleaned them up. The nanny stepped closer, her head at an angle. Lacey palmed a handful and tucked them into her pocket, then turned for the river. "We're more ready now, I think." She paused a half step while the nanny picked her pocket and mouthed the sweet reward.

"Good show. You go first and I'll pull up the rear with Hank. He'll keep them plenty motivated. This would be a good time for you to tell me something about yourself since we've got a long, slow walk down a narrow lane."

The kid goat bucked and tried to dart sideways but she coaxed him back with a carrot. "Okay. Do you want recent history or archival?"

"Well, I'm sure Luke filled your ears with stories about Wren and me when we were little, so how about some of that vintage? You know, brothers and sisters and what you played."

"I'm the first and last in the birth order of my family, though Mom claims they tried otherwise. Good thing my aunt lived just around the corner, so I could play with my three cousins whenever I wanted. We were pretty close until, one by one, we all ventured off to college. They still call and visit when we meet back in Omaha for the holidays."

"You're a cornhusker? Well, I never would have guessed that. I think I was in Omaha with a 4-H group as a kid, but all we saw was the inside of a livestock arena."

"They should have taken you guys to the zoo. It's truly incredible. I volunteered there every summer during high school."

"That's where your goat magnetism must have begun. Or maybe that was training to be a farm girl, and you just didn't recognize it." When she gave him a corrective look over her shoulder, he thought he might have pushed the idea a little too far.

"For your information, I've been reading a blog of the group called 'Women Managing the Farm' every night. It's quite entertaining as well as informative."

He pulled his goat pack up closer to hers and Hank circled the perimeter. The trail narrowed behind the corral and followed a hedgerow outside the pasture fence. "Maybe you could write up this river migration adventure and teach them how to bait and hook a captive audience."

Lacey ducked when a spider web appeared under a gnarled tree branch, which seemed to set off a string of lightning bugs ahead.

"Looks like the stars have dropped low on the trail this evening."

"Stars are fine, but spiders need to keep to themselves…"

"Aha. Do I detect a weak spot in the city girl's armor? A less valiant man would use that against you at some unguarded moment." He'd hoped to get a rise out of her. Another handful of carrots went into her back pocket. The nanny goat noticed.

When the kid begged for inclusion, Lacey held a couple in her palm for it to snatch. "But I wouldn't be walking with any less valiant man." She shot him a sharp glance under her knit brow.

"Point well taken. Hey, see that wood post coming up on the left? My grandpa left that in place when they re-set the pasture fence. In the old days, they used hedge tree posts that had little rot to them. Dad insisted he go modern with iron posts for the replacement fence, and did grandpa ever complain—mostly about the cost. Now look, that fence is even outlasting me." He hadn't meant for that last comment to have such a stinger of regret, but boy, he sure felt it.

She turned and walked backward a few steps. "I've always heard that it's a sign of good stewardship to leave things better than how you found them. If we don't have any guarantee on the duration, I suppose we should live like any day could be the last."

His goat herd mingled with hers as he caught up a few steps. One glimpse over her shoulder spoke of immediate trouble ahead.

"Hold it right there. Don't take another step." He grabbed a branch out of the hedgerow, lunged past her, and scraped a huge garden spider web out of her path. The large yellow and black creature clung to the branch, which he produced at arm's length.

She burrowed her face into his chest. When he tossed the branch back into the wayside, she glanced up at him in partial appreciation. "And I thought it a ploy to trick me into kissing you."

The kid goat climbed the back of her leg and helped itself to a carrot, which made him unable to keep from laughing any longer. After she shooed the goat away, she straightened with a defiant spark in her green eyes. A lightning bug went off near her shoulder and he took the whole scene in like something precious and vulnerable. "Oh, I'm holding back till we get to the river. But it's not that easy, trust me."

She walked away, dragging her little herd with Hank's help.

Wray whistled for the dog, which caused her to fire a kindled look over her shoulder that hit him like a dangling carrot. Too bad Grandpa's hedge post marked only the halfway point to the river, as they still had a far piece to go.

Chapter 16

The bow of the canoe slid effortlessly into the water beneath the overhanging bridge. Captivated, Lacey grabbed the gunwales and maneuvered her way forward, while Wray sat across the stern to make the boat more stable. She stepped over the seat and knelt on the hull. The boat dipped to one side, so she shifted her weight and leaned back on the seat for support. "Ready, captain. You can get in and shove us off."

The boat rocked and the push forward came right behind it. The dog whined as they departed dry land, and the antique vessel made its claim on the water. Lacey made a hurried reach for her paddle. She poled along in the shallows off the right side of the canoe. Minnows scattered at the interruption. They soon floated beyond the bridge's shadow into the open sun of a fine June day. A paddle clunked against the boat's stern.

Wray slid the cooler up behind the dog's perch.

"No leaks so far. That's a good sign." Secretive shorebirds took wing from a sandbar to the left and Hank yipped good riddance.

She enjoyed the feel of the boat under her knees and began to relax. "When you're with me, you have to stay positive."

"Okay, I will. Now any time your arm gets tired, feel free to switch sides. I'll alternate with you and J-stroke when I need to, as long as you don't overpower me, that is."

"I'll hold back then, because I typically like to start out strong."

"Remember that we're not in a hurry. Today we don't have a care in the world."

"That's not too shabby an attempt at recreation for a man who doesn't pretend."

"Thank you, bow-stroker. Sometimes I have helpful amnesia. It's a coping mechanism."

She scanned the riverbank. "As long as you don't forget me, I can deal with that." A cool ripple of water splashed across her back as the nose of the canoe changed direction. She would have posed an objection if it hadn't felt so refreshing. On its way to the mid-nineties, the day opened with a tint of cloudless cornflower blue. "Granted, I'm in the splash zone up here and I fully intended to get wet, so have your fun at my expense. Hey, watch the submerged log to the left." She reached out with her paddle and pushed off to avoid contact. The bow headed away from the obstacle.

"You're my eyes up there." Wray pulled a power stroke to send them downriver.

"Aye-aye, captain. I'll keep my eyes on the water up ahead."

"And I'll keep my eyes on you."

Like clockwork, the water play trickled across her back again. She launched a mock nuisance glare over her shoulder, just in time to see the incoming aerial attack. A blue blur swooped past and filled the air with a raspy rat-a-tat noise. She paddled on, her mouth open in admiration of the passer-by.

"Belted kingfisher," Wray said. "It's a true river resident, like me."

She shoved her sunglasses back in place between strokes. "Well, you have a better singing voice. The bird was pretty cute though, in a stocky-necked sort of way. It flashed lots of color and that's what I like—color." She nodded for emphasis and her ponytail bobbed under her visor strap.

He struck his paddle against the wooden canoe in a thump as though he'd been distracted. "And I like black, long black." His tone held a caress.

She smiled at the compliment and drew a full stroke off the point of the bow before she countered. "You're oh so obvious, Wray." She switched her paddle to rest her left shoulder.

"I'm just admiring nature's beauty, the same as you."

The wet back feeling returned as he shifted sides to match her. Lacey let the synchrony settle onto her shoulders where the paddling power originated. "Overhanging bush up ahead. Let's not admire it too up-close."

"A willow tree, not a bush. Sand bank willows are a dime a dozen along here. It might be dripping with snakes, but I wouldn't consider it a real menace for spiders. No worries."

"I wouldn't mind meeting a snake, as long as I see him before he sees me." The canoe angled away from the encroachment, and she rested a stroke while he steered. Beautiful along this stretch, the bank shifted high above the river and blocked all else from view. "This river is a place set apart, isn't it? No wonder you can come here and not have a care in the world. It's like a safe zone, safe from threats up on land, a place where you can just float along."

"And now you know my little secret. I'm glad you like it. That means a lot to me."

An idea came to her and she stretched for a bow reach to send them into a slight eddy. She pulled up onto the seat and switched around. The dog barked.

Wray shoved his hat up high on his forehead. "Uh-oh. Somebody's rocking the boat."

A bent willow cascaded shade over them as the boat drifted toward the shore. She giggled and stepped over the dog, her hands clamped on the sides of the boat as she went. "We're too far apart in this thing." She slid onto the cooler to rectify the matter.

He laughed and held his paddle down to anchor them against the river's flow. "Too far apart for what?"

She scooped up a handful of water and spilled it down her neck in an attempt to cool off. When Wray watched the drips work their way down the V-neck of her T-shirt, something caught in her throat when she tried to speak.   "Do I have to explain everything?" She leaned toward him and removed her sunglasses. Rewarded by his genuine look of surprise at the sneak attack, she slipped off the cooler and touched his knee.

"But the captain's on duty." He glanced up at an overhanging tree limb. A hidden bird sang a sharp note and then took wing above them. "This is *my* territory you're invading."

The dog barked in agreement but she had no intention of stopping her mutiny now. "I remember being kissed by you on the riverbank up in Hutch, and now turnabout is fair play." She pulled into striking distance.

Ever dutiful, Wray grabbed a handful of willow branches and pushed off with his paddle.

That maneuver set opportunity in motion. She tugged off her visor and dipped under his hat brim to land a premeditated kiss. The canoe circled around his grip on the tree and lent an extra sensation of dizziness to the embrace. Lacey hummed in contentment as she broke away, the scene of him so close filtered by her eyelashes. "Now navigate on, captain." She left him a coy smile as she turned and shifted forward past the cooler.

He released the willow branches and the canoe spun without true direction. "I forgot where I was going."

She stepped around the dog and patted its head. As she slid onto her caning seat, she knew what to recommend. "Just follow me." She grabbed her paddle and strung out an impressive set of strokes. Between the heat of the day, the exertion of paddling, and the afterburn of their embrace, she soon became overheated. She snatched off her T-shirt and made a modest adjustment to her bathing suit top. The boat shifted from the rear and she looked back to find the captain in a state of visual astonishment. She dipped the shirt into the water, balled it up and threw it at him. It landed as a direct blow on his chest. "Close your mouth or say something."

"Uh…wow?" His paddle soon thumped against the boat.

She swept with a bow stroke and pulled the craft out into the main flow. "Don't sink us on account of your distraction, captain. We have a turtle log to the left up ahead." Only the boat responded, as she had shipwrecked his nautical skills, at least for a while. She extended her paddle stroke into a bow sweep away from the turtle basking spot, which seemed to knock the turtles into the water, one by one. She giggled at the antics and cooling water soon splashed her bare shoulders as the man in the stern added his two cents. *Maybe being skittish is a good thing, especially if you're on the tip end of the log.* She rested the paddle on her knees and watched a silver-blue dragonfly dart above the water.

~

Wray took a moderate stroke to send the canoe through the cusp of the river's bend. Lacey had been quiet ever since he had challenged her to select their lunch spot. A straight stretch of river opened before them and exposed a lengthy sandbar to the west that held promise. He paddled through the scoured-out pool and struck something deep in the water. Its exodus created a ripple away from the boat.

Lacey pointed with her dripping paddle. "I like this sandy place over here. How about lunch in the shade of those trees along the back? I might need to be out of the sun for a little while."

"My knees need to straighten out, too." He dragged his paddle and made the canoe nose toward the sandy beach. Right before they ran aground, his canine friend launched for the shore. The ensuing splash created a clatter of wing beats as two great blue herons made their departure.

"Oh my word. That was outright beautiful," Lacey said. "Thank you, Hank, for flushing out the color."

Wray stepped into the shin-deep water and shoved the canoe up on dry land. When she stood with a wobble, he moved forward to offer her a steady hand.

He held her elbow as she stepped out. "It takes a second to get your land legs back. Good pick on the lunch spot, by the way. Don't think I've ever noticed this particular stretch before."

"Which will make it all the more memorable, since we're together." She wiped her hands on her shorts. "Let's explore before we get the picnic cooler out."

"Hank is already on scout duty, but we'll knock around behind him and see what's here." He grabbed his sneakers as her flip-flops plopped onto the sand. When he stepped up beside her, the sight of her bare shoulders made his empty stomach pang. "Hey, your shoulders look red. Maybe you should put your shirt back on until we've found some shade." He toed into the sneakers, a grit-filled reunion.

She reached for the shirt in the canoe. "My sunscreen may not have overpowered this glare."

He whistled for the dog and started walking in the opposite direction, to where the sandbar lengthened downriver.

Lacey ran up behind him and intertwined her fingers with his. The connection lasted all of six steps until she found an interesting root washed smooth by the river and now cast aside. She picked it up and turned it slowly in her hands. Turning, she peeked through the knothole and then peered over it at him. "I'm going to keep this driftwood as a memento of our first day on the river together," she said. "See how it ended up a thing of beauty even though it didn't start out that way?"

He caught the inference. Did it matter to her, knowing he sat poised on the edge of dispossession?

He opted to make light of it. "Let's hope we all have a pretty root anchored deep inside." The dog ventured out of the water's edge, shook to dry off, and coated their legs with sand and water. "Wow. Thanks, Hank. Run and play, boy." When he searched for a stick to throw, Lacey clutched the driftwood to her chest to keep it off-limits. Hank found a stick and began to escort them down the bar.

She pointed with the driftwood. "What's that in white up high there?"

"I have a feeling we're about to find out." She tried to bump his ribs with the souvenir, but he broke into a jog to explore the shrubby interior of the sandy bank. Several willows clustered, forming a high shady spot that caught his attention, as his stomach had been complaining with regularity.

"I'm not losing the race today," she said as she sailed by at full speed. "Loser pays," she called over her shoulder.

Unsure whether he had enough energy left to put up a good fight, he keyed his pace up a notch to make his attempt look realistic. As they got closer, he recognized the white cast on the bushes, especially once the round bloom pattern became discernible.

"Okay, you win." With his lungs on fire, he bent to catch his breath.

She propped the driftwood on her calf and examined the tiny white flowers covering the shrub. "I can hardly believe this. It's so amazing." She traced the ball-like blooms with her fingertips and pulled off her glasses. When her visor slid off, her hair fell loose.

Still hunched and winded, Wray looked up in time to witness the cascade. "You're right, it's amazing." With the honesty of discovery still in her eyes, something went liquid inside of him. A veil-like white backdrop surrounded her features, lending her the appearance of a gorgeous bride. His knees quaked and he could not shake either the vision or the feeling.

"Wray, you don't look so good. Maybe we should eat now and play later."

"Buttonbush," he said, accompanied by only a vacant stare.

"I never knew a man could be done in by a buttonbush." She took his hand and led him back toward the boat.

"Good shade over there." He nodded toward the willows.

She sidestepped to the trees and pulled him along with her. "Somebody needs to wait in the shade while I retrieve the picnic lunch. You pick a spot and I'll bring the towel and cooler." She released her grip with a final tug and sent his feet on a path toward the lunch spot.

He saluted, which earned him a giggle of relief, and plodded through the sand as he dodged tangles of catbrier and river-deposited debris along the way. Wray assessed his situation. Maybe being dazed by the sun had caused his loss of focus, but more likely he'd fallen moonstruck over the woman in the bow of his boat. Physical attraction he could deal with, but mirages of a marriage partner escalated the matter. The river somehow lost its meandering charm and became only a backdrop to what his heart could see. He entered the shade and leveled a suitable spot, but only because she would expect it. A man possessed by a clamor of the heart, he became a stranger to himself, wide open and vulnerable to attack.

~

Lacey propped against the cooler trying not to shift and awaken Wray from his post-lunch catnap. She studied his face with his squint lines now relaxed, enjoying his strong cheekbones and the curve of his jaw. He seemed content here by the river, at home and a part of it. Sleep managed to cancel the weight of the foreclosure and free him of its countdown. Tomorrow she would have to resurrect the subject and drop her news about the professional distancing the REO investigation had mandated. It would exact a momentary toll on the progression of their courtship, an unavoidable outcome. *How bad would the damage be?* Still, if she didn't help ferret out the wrong-doing, there would be a whole string of victims like Wray, and she would be part of the predator bank turning them into prey. For once, she could be part of the solution, even if it meant separation from the one thing she wanted the most.

It struck her that only God could work out something positive from a matter this convoluted, so she began to pray. The river's voice joined the unspoken request, and she rested in the repose until the dog barked by the water's edge.

She flinched and Wray awoke in her lap, his eyes blinking. "Tell me the first thing that comes to you mind," she said, her voice soft with attention.

He turned on his side and propped up on his elbow to look at her, his eyes tiny slits of blue haze. "You're a soft place to fall." He smiled but it flickered like a dragonfly's wings. He rested his forehead on the cap of her shoulder and she touched his sun-bleached hair. "I'm falling in love with you, Lacey… and I'm blaming that buttonbush over there."

She laughed at his improbable confession and the mix of nature that it evoked. "Blame me," she whispered. "Blame the breathless kisses and me always wanting to be out here in the country where you are. Blame baby goats and long black hair, haylofts full of stars, and a daisy bouquet. Everything seems to work against us—unless, of course, this is the way God meant for it to be."

"I can't fight it, but the Lord knows I've tried." He sat up and separated from her.

Lacey's heartbeat echoed in her ears. Would it end right here like a shipwreck in the sand, a voyage ill-fated and never sanctioned? That would represent the quickest answer to prayer she'd ever received. Short of breath, she turned green at the gills.

Wray stared out at the river, ever flowing nearby. "I don't know what this looks like, as there's a lot of shifting sand in my life right now…"

"I don't think this is about where we are, I think it's more about where we're going. It's a higher plane, this landscape of the heart."

He ran his fingers through his hair and seemed to struggle with her comment, but she held her peace. "River Ranch might not be part of the equation." An ounce of caution tainted his voice.

She folded her knees to her chest and wrapped her arms around her legs. "I'm in love with you, Wray…not the land. When I look at you, everything else fades into the background. I think we should give it a chance."

"You love me?" His gaze locked with hers. He leaned closer as though to study her further, like a bend in the river that hides what comes next.

She drew in a breath and didn't trust it, exhaled and released her legs. When his fingertips touched her neck, she couldn't think at all. She felt his stubble scrape as they went cheek-to-cheek, and the sensation further arrested her mind. A hostage of his heart with no means of escape, she turned to find his lips first and let the river sweep her away.

Chapter 17

Who's the romantic behind this double date?" Lacey froze, determined to know how it came about. Wren shifted in the booth and Luke's forearm flexed like he'd received a pinch under the table. Wray chuckled at the pair and downed half his glass of iced tea.

"We thought it'd be good just to be a couple without any other cares in the world," Wren replied. An honest blush made her eyes turn deeper blue.

Her answer tugged at Lacey's heart as she discovered a newfound appreciation for being genuine. As she glanced around the Carriage House restaurant, pie cabinets topped with gem-colored jelly jars echoed the sentiment. The lack of fancy made it all the more real, and her gaze met Wray's to solidify the effect.

Luke tucked his napkin into his lap. "Church lasted a half hour too long for this old sinner. Hope you guys get a piece of the first plate of chicken, as I could eat the whole bird. How about it, Wray? Are your ribs touching yet?"

"That canoe trip yesterday has made me hungrier than a grizzly bear." Wray pressed down his shirt front. "Time on the water always seems to do that to me."

"Some things never change," Wren said. "You've always been attached to that river, like it's your lifeline. At least we knew where to find you if something started festering in another department."

Lacey straightened her silverware as she tried to suppress a smile. He did have a natural ease on the river. She'd seen it.

"I wouldn't infer predictability for a man who took his goat herd to an auction and brought them right back home again," Wray teased, a gleam in his eye.

Wren worked her mouth into a pucker as she formulated her comeback. "Nobody's going to buy you off that river, brother. I'm sure of that."

A host of servers rushed the table next as they balanced several large platters loaded with the family-style meal. Lacey gasped at the large portions and glanced at Wray for some kind of justification.

Luke reached for the platter of fried chicken. "Hallelujah and welcome to food heaven."

Wray landed a second hand on the platter and forced his friend to center it between them. Wren accepted the creamy mashed potatoes and Lacey took the green beans, leaving room for the rolls on the outer rim of the table. A pewter gravy bowl found the tabletop along with butter and a jar of honey.

"Somebody ask the blessing before I fall into sin again because I've got to have me some of that chicken pretty quick," Luke said.

"Dear Father," Wray replied a little on the loud

side. "We don't deserve this moment or this good food but we're grateful for it down to the soles of our feet. Help us relish the time we have together and fit us for your service."

"Amen," Luke added. He reached for the largest chicken breast on the plate.

Lacey lost track of what happened next, as Wray leaned close for their usual method of benediction. When she pulled back from Wray's quick peck, she witnessed Luke extend the same greeting to Wren, even though the chicken breast hovered about chin height in his hands.

Wren spooned a generous heap of fluffy potatoes onto Luke's plate. "That truly makes me think of heaven." She partook of the green beans and passed them across the table.

"Much obliged," Luke managed, a hunk of meat hanging from his mouth. An exaggerated wink followed and Wren cleared her throat, visibly affected by his attention.

When Wray shifted the meat platter toward her, Lacey pulled it within reach with a warm smile. The world shrank to the size of a dining booth, both savory and endearing all at the same time.

~

Wray stepped toward a large blue bloom on a spike. "Perimeter checks seem to be a good match for a lazy Sunday afternoon."

Lacey followed his lead and bent to touch a stem that had already gone to seed in a series of puffy blisters. "Blue wild indigo?" She tested the seedpod with a squeeze between her thumb and index finger.

He nodded with a smile. Her earnestness to become

familiar with the prairie tickled him. "It'll rattle in the wind when the seeds dry. By then, I'll miss the blue out here. Come September, everything will be yellow-gold as far as the eye can see." He gazed at the horizon and traced the fence line around the pasture.

"Should we go check that corner post? It'll help us walk off that heavy lunch."

"Might as well touch the corners just to say we did. It looks like the daisy fleabane is trying to take over out here. Maybe I should have rested this pasture earlier."

"Or make plans to rotate the herd more often next year," she suggested, weaving her fingers into his. "I learned that on my farm woman blog."

A smile tucked into his cheek and he realized how happy she made him. "Somebody is really getting into this rural life thing." He pulled her closer until their shoulders touched. "That's got a good feel to it, even though you're much more optimistic than I am concerning next year." Thoughts of his inadequate bank balance and his niece's rising medical bills flitted through his mind and he blinked them away so she couldn't read his worry.

"You're going to beat your NOD countdown, Wray." She crinkled her nose. "The wheat crop looks great—you said so yourself when we pulled in."

"That's true, and if the market holds, I can sell right away. That beats the first of September by a long shot. There are a few 'ifs' along the way, but it should happen." They approached the far western fence line and he slowed his stride to allow her time to respond.

"My bets are on you and River Ranch." Her hand joined his to touch the rough stone. "Let's stop and say a little prayer right here, and ask Jesus for it. He's our redeemer over all life's trials, so we should surrender this foreclosure to him."

Fascinated at the sensation of having someone believe in him, let alone a helpmate around the farm, he stepped closer. He removed his hat and shaded both their faces with it. "Ask for me, will you? Maybe I'm too close to the ledge and can't talk about it like I should. I've tried to be a good steward, even if it doesn't look like it from the outside. Pleasance has to come first right now. That's my commitment." His voice grew too husky to continue, so he braced against the corner post and closed his eyes.

A meadowlark sang from down the fence line as Lacey's hand found the post between his. "Dear Heavenly Father, we relinquish this farm to your care, as neither Wray nor I know how this foreclosure is going to turn out. But we ask you to work the outcome to our mutual good, and that we might be stronger as individuals and together as a couple in the aftermath. In your divine provision, we ask that you bring the wheat in at its full yield, and that Wray would get a good price for it when he sells. And please make it be in time for the redemption period on River Ranch. In the power of Jesus Christ we pray…"

"Don't say 'amen.' Please don't let it end." A sob broke his request. Something shook him to his core, despite his attachment to the post. The thought of the land being snatched from under him became too much to bear in the moment, and he trembled at the realization that he might not be able to stop the process. God could, but only if he wanted to intervene.

"No one's saying 'amen,' Wray," Lacey replied, her voice confident and comforting. Her arms slid around his back and held him close.

Insecurity crashed over him in stark severity. Another sob shook him as he snuffed out the rising tears on her sturdy shoulder. Here on the westernmost point of the ranch, he began to fall apart under the strain of suffering and a downward ticking clock. Through the fog in his brain he could barely hear her whispers.

"A broken heart is dear to God." She caressed the back of his neck.

"We don't have to say 'amen' then." His lips traced her high cheekbone and alighted on her wet eyelashes for a kiss. He kissed the bridge of her nose next and studied her beauty up close. Almost dizzy with emotion, he had one last statement he wanted to make, so he held his urge off for a long second and slid a hand up under her ponytail. "If this is love, then I'm crazy for it." The distance between them closed. The kiss lasted through the meadowlark's song and then some. A quiet power filled his chest. His resolve had returned.

~

For the first time, Lacey sensed the gentle slope of the land as it fell away toward the river. The second stone post stood in the corner as they approached. Wray had grown quiet since his meltdown across the pasture. The sun seemed to drop with determination, a cue she was running out of time to discuss her bank situation with him. She drew an exaggerated breath as he checked the fence. When he bent to touch the bottom strand, she waited for an explanation.

He stood and presented her with a bent metal fastener that evidently had worked loose. "You see this? Someone is taking my fence apart." His tone became sharp and accusatory. He strode to the next iron post and, again, the bottom wire was unfastened. "These clips don't just fall off by themselves. This dismantling is intentional. I'm calling Sheriff Earhart when we get back to the farmhouse. He can document this tampering." Anger set his jaw as he walked the fence line counting the number of posts where the clips had been unfastened.

Frozen in place, a dread came over Lacey and wedged between her ribs. She couldn't let the sheriff see her with Wray for the same reason the bank wouldn't let her continue to date him. She could no longer remain involved personally and work to expose the fraud professionally. But the bank wouldn't have caused the fence situation. That aspect had her truly perplexed. One thing was certain. She would need to level with Wray before he made that phone call to the sheriff. Watching his posture turn rigid as he walked the fence line sealed the deal. That man didn't possess an ounce of pretend, which meant she had to lay the mandated separation out in the open and step away. She would help the bank, at least through the end of his redemption period. After that, she had something more important to redeem.

~

"This will only take a minute." He slammed the door behind his guest. A man with a mission, he skipped up the kitchen steps to find the phonebook. The kitchen drawer opened with a protest, but he yanked it into compliance, determined to make the call. He lifted the phonebook out and flipped open the front cover. His fingertips traced over the emergency numbers handwritten onto the blank roster. He located the sheriff's number and reached for the phone.

Lacey stepped in and blocked the way.

"Come on. Let me get this done." He could only be patient to a point. When she refused to move, he noticed that her face had blanched white. "Lacey? Is something wrong?"

"Wray, we need to talk—before you call the sheriff." Her gaze dropped. "Could we sit down at the table for a minute? This isn't going to be easy for me." She tried to work a lump down her throat.

Startled, he released his hold on the phonebook. "You talk and I'll listen." He turned his chair backwards and sat across it, his elbows propped on the chair back. He no more wanted to halt his momentum than the man in the moon, but something obviously bothered her.

"This is about my work at the bank," she said, her fingertips pressed together. She lifted her gaze to regard him directly. "Remember how you challenged me once to consider the other side of the fence—the side where I could be an advocate for the foreclosure client instead of the agent of condemnation?"

"Yeah, I think that would be a better fit for you, honestly, but do we have to talk about it right now?"

"Yes, because I've been offered a chance to do exactly that, right at Fidelis Bank. I want you to know that I've decided to take the offer. I'm not at liberty to tell you any of the specifics, except that I'll be integrated into the REO group for better documentation of how they operate through the foreclosure process."

"You mean to flush out anything not kosher?" Uncomfortable with the whole idea, he rubbed the back of his neck to stop his skin from crawling. "This has something to do with that surveyor's card in my door, doesn't it?"

She shifted in her seat and glanced around the kitchen. "Let's consider the card a catalyst for the bank to do some internal investigating on procedural lapses that might be taking place. There's a glaring reason I cannot discuss this with you further, Wray."

"Because it's happening to me? And you're now investigating my case?" His gaze intensified. "And now I need to guess why you're telling me this *before* I make the call to the sheriff and ask him to come out."

Her hands pressed flat against the table and her lips drew into a thin line. Seconds ticked by and she held her peace.

His patience boiled over. "Go ahead and tell me, Lacey. Get it out on the table and let me deal with it."

Her expression cooled. "To lend my professional investigation the credibility it will need in court, I have to curtail our personal relationship for the duration of the redemption period for River Ranch. Mr. Alderman, the bank's president, set forth the conditions of the investigation and I had to choose in or out, no negotiating in between."

The numbness started in his chest and pulsed upward to his brain. His thoughts short-circuited and rendered him speechless.

"There will be more victims after you, Wray. Lots more." Lacey leaned across the table. "Someone has to step in and break the chain. After lots of prayer and soul-searching, I know that someone is me."

"What about you and me?" He struggled for breath as though his lungs leaked.

"We'll pick up right where we left off come the first of September. You'll have redeemed the ranch from the Notice of Default by then, and I will have the procedural review wrapped up in a neat legal package. There may be several more cases down the pike afterwards, but they won't require the isolation your case demands."

He stood, rankled by the news and uneasy about the separation. "Oh, I'm a case now, am I?" He ran his fingers through his hair. "Excuse me, I thought we were in love here. And now you're pulling out."

"Nothing has changed in my heart, Wray…"

"Why did you even come out here this weekend? You knew the whole time, didn't you?"

"I came to prove to myself that what I felt is real—and it is. You confessed it first but I knew that even this assignment, as difficult as it might be, wouldn't stand between us if we were in love. Eight weeks will pass like seconds compared to the time we'll share afterward. Keep your perspective on the long term and the higher plane of what's just and right."

He heard her, he understood her words, but he could not accept her message in his heart-of-hearts. Turned into a victim two times over, the bank plan churned his stomach and soon boiled his blood. Rebellion started in his boots as he strode for the backdoor, desperate for fresh air. He kicked the door harder than he should have and the reverberation shook through him. *So this is love?* He aimed for the elm with his head on fire and his hands quaking like a willow in the wind.

~

Lacey caressed the tea towel over the last plate and put the dish back into the cupboard. She had insisted on a light dinner before she left but it had been a hollow affair. Wray had sat across from her, quiet and introspective, barely contributing to simple conversation at the table. Their last meal together had turned into mush.

He bustled around the kitchen area aimlessly. At last he pulled some hardware from the junk drawer for an invisible project in the sunroom. Anything to get away.

She stepped into the dining room and turned on the buffet light to enjoy the color palette of tiny birds one more time before she left. In a melting pot of emotions, the colors blurred into a stained glass pattern she would have to remember for two long months. Somewhere behind her, a radio cut on to a sad song.

"How about we put some hay out for the goats before you leave?" Wray stood in the doorway. His voice lacked any sense of play.

The request landed on her heart like a perfunctory chore. "Sure," she replied as she wiped a tear from her cheek. She stepped to the buffet and turned off the light inside, trying to hold onto the image. When he led her out to the barnyard without even offering a hand to hold, she took it as entirely her fault. She had hurt him and now didn't know how to make it all better.

The elm's outline hunched over dusk's last glimmer and she followed without a word to the feed room off the back of the lean-to. She stepped in behind him and his presence filled the space, sweet hay scents swirling in the air. He turned with the hay and she moved back against the doorframe, aching for his touch as he passed by unaware.

By the gate, Wray pulled the hay into pads and slung them over the top rail. He stood at the gate like he was going to say something, but must have thought better of it. He brushed the hay off his shirt and turned for the house.

She fed a handful to the kid goat and rubbed her palm over its bony forehead until it lost interest. It cannot end this way, she determined. She stepped back into the sunroom to trap her heartache. A male singer on the radio begged for a good night ending, over and over. His duet partner alternated her verse, also longing for his sweet embrace at the door. *How ironic.*

She gathered her things, the hollow farewell flattened by strategic betrayal. Wray appeared above her, backlit by the solitary light bulb she had washed dishes under. The music pulsed as the singing couple worked it out and met each other halfway.

He stepped down into the dark sunroom and grabbed her bag from her without a word. When she stumbled back against the screen door, he collapsed and pressed her there like a super magnet, an explosion of emotional heat.

She dropped everything at his touch and embraced him in the fallout as though her very life depended on it. Their kiss raged on with a desperate edge until the whole thing fell ragged on the heels of nightfall, abandoned in a whimper that came from her own throat.

Chapter 18

Wray stepped to the phone as it rang the third time. He'd hoped it would be Lacey but knew that wasn't possible. Five days of silence had already stretched between them. He chafed at the lonesomeness it left. Hank whined and he patted the Border collie with his free hand as he captured the phone with the other.

"River Ranch." He glanced out the back door of the sunroom. A woman's voice started to speak across the line but backed out and he heard a faint "I can't" confession in the background. Someone else took the phone and his senses shifted to high alert.

"This is Luke, Wray. Wren wants you to know we've brought Pleasance to the hospital on the west side of Wichita." A pause followed. "It doesn't look good at this point. The doctor is in with her now."

"What about her latest chemo treatment? Didn't that make any difference?" He leaned against the counter. The dog met his gaze with sad eyes and worked its head back under his free hand. He heard his question being repeated in the background but the response was inaudible.

Luke continued. "Her little body's been through too much. She doesn't seem to be able to keep up the fight anymore. Wren says she's made her peace with it and hopes you can, too."

He squeezed his eyes closed to shut out the reality of her situation. He couldn't stomach that she was slipping away from him. The first little darling he'd known from birth, his niece had captured his heart with her doll baby smiles and precious childhood antics. Given his romantic isolation now, severance of this connection proved too much.

"Tell Wren I'll be right there, Luke. Ask her if I can bring anything."

"Hold on a minute." He relayed the message. "She asks if you can bring your Bible. She would like to read some scripture to Pleasance when it quiets down some."

"I'll do it, brother. Do you need anything?" A long pause followed as the caller withheld his response. Wray's mind began working a mile a minute, thinking about what he needed to do before he drove into town. The dog wiggled under his hand and he caressed its head with a newfound tenderness.

"You know what I need." Luke left the conversation open-ended.

"Hold her for me until I can get there." Wray released the phone like it was to blame. His boots scuffed across the kitchen floor and he looked at the carnage he'd left in the sink all week, like some sort of domestic rebellion. Disgust filled his throat and he pushed the faucet open to run water over his hands. He wouldn't enjoy this particular trip to town in the least. Under normal circumstances, Lacey would join him and share the weight of the suffering. But his life was the furthest thing from normal he could imagine. The ticking clock represented a tightening thumbscrew that was sure to bring nothing but pain. And the hurt had already started.

~

Lacey sat at her laptop trying to forget what Friday night typically held. She should be slung across a hayloft staring at the stars beside the most handsome rancher on the planet. Instead, she sat suffocating here in her overpriced apartment in the middle of a concrete-clad city. She pulled up her e-mails, anxious to see if she'd had any response to her inquiries on Wray's behalf. Time would only be meaningful if it brought some resolution to his dilemma, and she would exhaust every avenue possible to help him find a way out. She worked down to the reply from the Black Insurance Agency and double clicked with attitude.

"Dear Ms. Woodhouse." She read aloud, each word searing into her psyche. "Thank you for your recent inquiry into the coverage of Wray Benson's farm. According to my records, no claim has been filed on the two vehicles you documented as being destroyed in the grain elevator explosion, although I do see indications that they were discontinued from coverage the following year. For your accounting ledger, the International would be valued at $27,000 and the Ford truck would represent $21,000 in settlement value. Since Fidelis Bank currently holds a lien on the property, I can forward you a check for the combined amount by the end of the month. Please let me know how to proceed with this matter. Black Insurance Agency regrets any problems for our client that may have resulted from this omission. Please accept our apology, and I look forward to hearing back from you soon."

She pushed the desk chair back and stood in full victory mode. Next, she danced around the dining table with her fists punching the air. Wray had been so distraught at losing his parents in the grain elevator catastrophe, he had failed to recapture the insured value of the trucks destroyed that day. The money to help redeem River Ranch now appeared seemingly from nowhere, as though his father had been holding it for him all this time. In her jubilant celebration, her hip swiped the table's edge and glass slid on impact. Instinctively, her hands reached down to steady the masterpiece-in-the-making—her rendition of the flower-filled meadow at Wray's farm.

Warm thoughts of him coursed through her and she wrapped her arms across her chest, aware of what this money would mean to his struggle to regain the farm. She would talk to Julie first thing Monday morning and get her to authorize the transfer of funds. That should halt the NOD. Wray would pop out of the process free and clear. River Ranch would be saved.

First, she needed to reply back and request the belated settlement. A rush came over her at being in the position of advocacy and able to deliver good news, not condemnation. "Dear Lord, I think I'm going to like the other side of the fence." She hit the reply icon as she forced herself to sit down and focus.

The chandelier's illumination glinted off the stained glass work and it caught her peripheral vision.

"You are next, my fine friend. And I don't care if I stay up all night getting your daisies in the right spot. I'm on fire for the prairie and loving it. I simply love it!" As her heart soared, she thought of Wray and stopped to blow a kiss over the meadow depiction. Her eyes searched the desktop and she realized for the first time that she didn't have a snapshot of him to bide her over until they met again. "Not exactly great planning in the love department, dearie, though your detective work gets an A plus." The adrenalin rush lasted well past midnight, when she finally surrendered to her unmade bed.

~

"My niece is in the hospital dying," Wray confessed into his hands, his elbows propped on his knees. A murmur of support came from his classmates as the Sunday school teacher closed the distance between them and laid a comforting hand on his shoulder. For three days now, his nerves had stayed on jagged overload. The heaviness had grown unbearable.

"Let's hold off on our other requests for the moment and come around Wray to lift him up," Gene said.

Wray squeezed his eyes closed and held his hands over his face in an effort to conceal his turmoil, as chairs slid back in response to the request. Several heavy hands came in contact with his shoulders as the class members formed a scene out of the New Testament church. The even voice of the leader broke the plane of his silent struggle and he took limited solace in his words as the prayer started heavenward.

The petition was an earnest one, plainspoken and heartfelt, with pauses that were filled with expressions of agreement and thanks from the members around him. The burden lifted off of him toward the end, and he sensed something that felt like salvation and smelled like kitchen spices. At the "amen" he turned to find Lacey as she returned to her seat behind him, her face radiant and her eyes loving him in secret. She pressed a finger subtly to her lips and everything but the spasm of joy that sailed through his veins managed to quiet. She had come to be with him, albeit in public anonymity and a little distant. Times being what they were, he could accept that. The lesson that followed was lost on him, as he had already received his take-away for the day.

~

Lacey filed into the auditorium with the intention of sitting as far away from Wray as she could. A cool hand clasped her elbow and there stood little Miss Cora. She beamed a smile and shoved a bulletin at her. As they walked up the aisle, the aged greeter delivered her to Wray's pew and motioned her in. Lacey's mouth dropped open to form a protest, though it wasn't too forthcoming.

"Sit here with us, Miss Cora—we need a chaperone between us today." Wray moved down the pew cushion.

The widow's eye sparkled at the invitation and she flapped her stack of bulletins at him. "Let me go get rid of these," Cora replied. "Bessie Mae can cover for me and catch the stragglers."

Lacey sat primly on the cushion's edge against the end of the pew and glanced at the podium where the speakers took their places. Wray bent toward her and passed his bulletin for her inspection. The organ sounded its first notes the moment Cora returned, her fifties-vintage purse knocking against Lacey as she stepped past her to sit beside Wray. She finally took a glance at his hand-scrawled message across the top and let it filter down her loneliness.   Holding it to her chest, she took a constricted breath as the worship leader signaled everyone to rise. She found her feet but refused to release the bulletin and the bond between them that it bore. The first praise chorus ended with her mascara in total ruins. And to think she had come to buoy him up. What a laughable attempt, in a crying sort of way.

~

Monday dawned and the light that filtered into his easternmost window told Wray to get up, but his body felt like lead. Images blurred around the room and he rubbed his eyes to clear the picture. The vacant farm was too quiet. Now he missed the rooster waking him in its pre-dawn exuberance. Too much had changed, with more to come. He'd stayed up late looking at his finances and the total fell short by a long shot. The hospital stay would eat into his upcoming wheat sales and there wouldn't be enough left to make a sizable contribution to redeem the farm. Debt had become a bottomless pit into which all his resources and hopes could be thrown, and still it wouldn't be satiated. He rolled out of bed with a moan answered by a whimper from the dog outside his door.

"I'm coming, boy—little by little." He pulled the door open and a tail thumped the floor in unconditional love. "Morning, Hank. Let's go assault the outdoors." The dog sprang into action, high-tailing it to the kitchen door. He had no more released the screen door handle when the phone rang. He stumbled back up to the kitchen, raking his hair into place.

"River Ranch."

"The end's near, Wray." Luke's voice fell off the receiver, even and slow. "The doctor thinks you should come on out. It won't be long."

He covered his gasp as the news trickled down to his heart, although his mind had already clicked into gear.

"Let me shower and I'll be right out," he promised. "How's Wren?"

"Taking it one day at a time—like always. Don't wait, Wray."

He lowered the receiver while the dog scratched the door to get back in. He wished he could have learned how to do a better job of that as he glanced at the countdown calendar on the kitchen wall. A substantial string of days had already been crossed through, but there were many more hollow red boxes to go in his redemption period. A more important clock wound down today, and he would face it alone. The dog filed past and went straight to its food bowl. Operating on autopilot, Wray stopped long enough to fill the herder's dish. At least one of them should eat today.

~

"What do you mean, that's not possible?" Lacey's voice rose in disbelief. She stared at Julie and then the bank president, both standing rigid and in collusion. "How can you not accept the insurance money as a redemption deposit? This is truly beyond me." Though her attire gleamed professionalism, her attitude grew a bit testy. This was River Ranch, after all, and she had an emotional investment, try as she might not to show it.

"Please sit down, Ms. Woodhouse, and I'll explain it to you as best I can," Mr. Alderman replied.

Her knees stiffened in momentary refusal, but Julie gave her a sympathetic look, so she gave in and perched on the leather guest chair. Patience was not a virtue in her pocket today, making confrontation a rough way to start the week.

"There's been a complication, Lacey. Try to have some forbearance as we work through this together," Julie said as Mr. Alderman got comfortable behind his desk. At his cue, she sat in the second guest chair and folded her hands in the lap of her two hundred dollar suit.

Lacey looked down at her power-broker high heels and fought the urge to throw one against the walnut paneling.

"We're obligated by law to allow the foreclosure to run its full course, Ms. Woodhouse. You see, the sheriff came to see me late Friday and the news wasn't good. There has been additional tampering with the perimeter fence around the River Ranch pastures."

"I became aware of that on my last visit out, before we began this endeavor," Lacey replied, her words selected with caution. Julie's mouth twitched, which she knew was a nervous tick, clueing her that she wasn't the only one in the room extremely uncomfortable.

"So you can see how this marries up to what we're finding out within our own REO department, can't you?" He attempted to lead her into compliance.

A fire of indignation started in her lungs as she transformed into dragon lady. "We're inexplicably ahead in River Ranch's foreclosure schedule and applying pressure that shouldn't be there." She steadied herself. "There are three more cases following the same accelerated process, all of which I've documented in my daily e-mails back to you both."

"Good job, Lacey. We want you to know that you're doing just what we need to get this recorded, so we can put a halt to it," Julie said. Mr. Alderman nodded his appreciation of her comments and seemed hesitant to reveal his next tactic.

Lacey's skin began to crawl under her silk blouse. She tried to anticipate the manner of the complication but couldn't come up with it for the life of her. The room turned stifling.

"The sheriff knows the area well, and has known the rural families for several generations," Mr. Alderman said.

At the word "rural" something seized in Lacey's chest.

"It seems that Mr. Benson's neighbor to the west, a man named Darold Henley, may have more than just an aggressive interest in obtaining the adjoining foreclosed property come September."

"Brace yourself," Julie added.

Her mouth dropped open at the blatant warning. Lacey knew someone had tampered with the westernmost fence. She could close her eyes and visualize the neighboring farmhouse.

"Lacey?" Mr. Alderman called her back into the conversation. He stood and handed her a black and white photograph of a tombstone with a hyphenated family name. The inscription read "Henley-Odom" on it as clear as a bell. An alarm screamed inside her head as the onerous collusion came together for the first time.

"Wray's neighbor, Darold Henley, and your supervisor, Harold Odom, are half-brothers, Lacey," Julie stated, spelling it out. "Henley intends to use Odom's inside connections to leverage Wray into early foreclosure so he can put a low bid on the property and obtain it for a dime above the payoff amount."

Lacey froze in utter disbelief.

"Thus the scam deepens, and the bank is caught right in the middle of it," Mr. Alderman admitted. He seemed to pale with genuine remorse.

"The sheriff is convinced that we need to let the foreclosure action unfold all the way to its finger-pointing conclusion so we can get the conviction to stick in court," Julie said.

Unable to stop the gasp escaping her lips, Lacey shot up from the chair. There had to be some middle ground. With her fists clenched at her sides, she stepped toward the door, wanting to run from the reality and her part in it.

"Can we count on you to see this thing through, Lacey?" Julie hitched her plucked brow in anticipation.

Mr. Alderman followed with a pleading look. He folded his hands as if nothing more could be done.

Furious and brokenhearted at the same time, she stood simmering at the door. "Think of what this will do to Wray, could you? For even a minute? He'll be evicted from the only home he's ever known—it will be a sham for us, but blinding reality for him."

"We know you'll make it up to him, Lacey. That's our ace in the hole and the only reason we're asking you to go through with this," Julie replied. "You can redeem the damage done to Wray after the fact."

"Here's my one condition, and I'm absolutely set on this," Lacey countered. Her words came out with resolute fire. "On the last day of the redemption period, unknown to anyone else, I will be allowed to redeem the mortgage and save River Ranch. Otherwise, I'm not your player."

Julie turned ashen and deferred to the bank's senior officer.

"You have my word," Mr. Alderman replied.

Lacey sobbed and escaped into the hall, while a safety net of faith secured her plummeting heart.

Chapter 19

The second of July arrived hot as a pepper pod, and Wray knew he had to get with it despite his lack of motivation. Nothing seemed the same since Pleasance had slipped away, but the wheat stood ready for harvest according to God's perfect timing, and Luke was on his way to River Ranch to drive the grain truck for him. He sighed and shoved the combine shed door open which revealed the monstrous green machine that could save his ranch.

Barring any mechanical setbacks, he would cut for two days straight even into the night and get done by the upcoming holiday. Luke had already told him not to worry if harvest ran into Independence Day, because Wren could bring their picnic right there by the farm field and celebrate like generations before them had. Maybe hard work would bring him back to life and at least give his body purpose, even if his heart rode rock-numb inside his chest.

As he lifted a foot to the combine's ladder, his

mind wandered to Lacey. The bank would take Friday off for the holiday. As he opened the cab, the acrid mothball smell sliced away any fond sentiments, and he braced himself for the meticulous process of operating the combine. Farming was his deal anyway, and he would execute it fully to make a stab at staving off the foreclosure. With no fall crop coming behind wheat harvest, he wasn't sure he could maintain payments through the winter, as his reserve had been left bone dry. He'd cross that bridge when he came to it.

Wray hit the ignition and the choke simultaneously, making the sleeping giant shake and roar to life. He checked the gauges and sited on his clearance through the shed door, then inched the combine into the light of day. Under direct light, dust flew from every flank, another reminder that he lived in an imperfect world. Once the rear of the vehicle passed free and clear, he killed the ignition and descended the ladder to start the lubrication prep on the moving parts.

How many times had he helped his father, the two of them working in unison to cover both sides of the mammoth piece of equipment? He faced it alone now, although help waited in the wings. The Yoder meat truck would drop Luke by the grass farm on the edge of K-96, and he'd be there to pick up his grain truck driver, a fake smile in place. He tore the grease gun from the built-in toolbox and headed for his first point of inspection. The dog appeared around the front wheels, wagging its tail.

"Here we go, Hank, starting another wheat harvest," Wray said, full of mock enthusiasm. The dog responded with a bark, and somehow he didn't feel so alone.

~

Lacey slowed for the little town of Sabetha on the Kansas-Nebraska border, feeling confident that taking the extra day off to venture home had been the right thing to do. Two men hammered together a temporary fireworks stand along the roadside and she tossed them a wave as she passed. While seeing her parents served as reason enough for the visit, an ulterior motive drove her back home.

Wray's insurance settlement came in earlier in the week. She'd managed to secure it in an interest-bearing account in his name, while the bank withheld it from their REO unit for the sake of the investigation. She was still waiting to hear from the Mennonite Relief Fund regarding the payout on burial expenses for his parents. According to Wren, resident victims had been compensated at the time of the disaster to defray funeral costs. Why the Bensons had not been entitled to similar treatment, she was unsure, but it was worth a try. She'd felt obligated, as Wray's bank advocate, to attempt recovery.

She passed the edge of town and saw nothing but Nebraska cornfields beyond. Her parents had been supportive about her move to Wichita. They had been down to visit once, over Easter weekend, but she didn't think they had found the town too charming. Riverwalk had been in full spring bloom and they had strolled beside the teeming Arkansas River, swollen from recent rains. The thought of the river made her smile, and Wray popped into mind. Of course, the river always made her think of him. Lately everything seemed to revolve around him. That wasn't a bad thing, she assured herself, as she accelerated out into flanks of shoulder-high corn.

Asking her parents to advance the wedding fund might take some doing, but they had always said the money would be hers whenever she wanted it. With Wray's assets frozen at the bank, she would need it sooner than later. And it wouldn't be for a wedding—although she wouldn't object if one came thrown in with the package deal. No, the money would be for land, and for the redemption of a rancher who more than deserved it. The bank had promised her the opportunity to offer the redemption, and now what she needed equated to cold, hard cash.

Ask her parents for money suddenly struck her as sophomoric. Her savings account would be much stouter if her rent didn't run so high. That apartment had to go. She'd cancel her lease when it expired in August. Where would she go after that? The hayloft crystallized as a desirable solution, and her lips curled into a smile as she contemplated the possibility. Despite its lack of running water, the neighborhood had allure, and the manager seemed to cater to her comfort. Try as she might, she couldn't get the prospect out of her mind.

"Guide me, Lord. Help me make this request of my folks, and please let them say yes, for Wray's sake. And help me not to project myself into the scene—or what's best for Wray, if that's not your plan. Don't let me be presumptuous, only let me be obedient to your will. Most of all, help me undo the suffering that the bank must inflict on him, even though I don't know how to begin to do it—beyond loving him through. In the power of Jesus, I pray…" She stopped before amen came out, a poignant reminder of their relationship. The corn scenery blurred in a quenching mist of tears, which formed but never fell. In the peace that followed, a plan came to her for approaching her parents that made total sense. She could hardly wait to get there.

~

Luke nodded at the second half of the southernmost field. "Wheat looks good."

The auger worked above their heads as Wray emptied out the hopper for the ninth or tenth time. He'd lost track, but could retrace it later with the grain elevator receipts.

"It's pushing two o'clock, Wray. Let's stop long enough to eat the sandwiches Wren sent with me. Otherwise, I'll be in hot water when she comes tomorrow."

"Fair enough. I wouldn't want the only helper I have to get scalded." He let the tease free-fall, never breaking eye contact with the grain flow. "How about grabbing the cooler and riding a round with me? My cab's got air conditioning and your truck doesn't…"

"Be right back then." Luke climbed down the ladder under the auger's shadow. Tiny bits of chaff lofted in the breeze and rained down around him as he scurried to the far side of the truck.

Wray shoved the auger lever back and forth to clear the last few grains and tucked the auger back into place alongside the combine. Luke reappeared with a red cooler in tow and was back up on the deck in seconds. He unlatched the side door and welcomed his companion. No sooner had the man sat down when he swung the combine hard right and ate up the distance back to the standing wheat.

"One more time around ought to fill the load."

Wray took the napkin Luke offered. He wiped his hands clean and then rested the napkin on his lap. As a sandwich appeared, he looked down to check the header's height and engage the roller bar. He accepted the lunch offering and bit into the feast. Eating on the go set off a host of emotion-packed memories. He cleared his throat and looked over at his accomplice. "How long have we been eating this same lunch at harvest?"

Luke captured an oversized bite and tucked it into his cheek with a nod. "Remember how your dad had to have his with horseradish smeared all over?"

"Yeah. I told him his taste buds died when he turned forty," Wray replied. When no sharp jab of pain rode on the reminiscing, it pleased him. In tribute, he lifted the bologna sandwich in a triumphant gesture and made a third of it disappear.

"You mother's pickle spears were my absolute favorite." Luke cleared his throat with a long drink of water. "Hope Wren knows how to make those."

"She can do anything she sets her mind to—with mixed results, of course." A smile broke free when he saw Luke blush a bit. "You two must be getting serious, talking like that." Wray demolished the remainder of his sandwich, all the while focused on the field.

Luke held his peace as the ripened wheat rolled onto the scythe and fell against the roller. "You know that roast beef dinner that will follow harvest up at my place?"

Wray nodded, his elbows flying to make the right angle turn down toward the river.

"Now lower your bar a tad as the land drops away."

"Backseat driver…what about the roast beef dinner?"

"I plan to ask Wren if she'll marry me after dinner, that's what," Luke replied. "I think she's ready, now that she's properly mourned—and I know I am."

Wray broke his gaze on the wheat field to make eye contact with his rider as if to gauge his sincerity. A gleam of hope flickered in the man's eyes, a gleam that reflected a deeper sentiment.

Luke adjusted the sandwich in his lap. "It's time for life to go on in a positive direction. I'll take care of her and the boy, I'll be privileged to, in fact."

"No question, Luke. You certainly have my permission for the hitch-up." Wray lowered the header as the land sloped further down. "Let me know how I can help—if she says 'yes,' that is." The tease curled a slight smile across his face and he turned again to make sure Luke knew he was kidding. A comfortable silence followed.

Luke balanced his half-eaten sandwich in both hands. "How about standing up with me as my witness, for one thing. I always wanted to come in on horseback. You wouldn't have a problem with that, would you?"

"Count me as your shadow, cowboy style or not." Wray slowed the combine for the lower corner.

Luke took a bite and seemed lost in thought. "I might buy Joshua a pony so he can ride in with us. Wouldn't that make a mother proud?"

"More than proud. She'll be bawling." He focused on the tight turn and eased into the header adjustment along the lower cut line. Finally satisfied, he leaned back to find an apple being offered.

"This one is store-bought, but you know your sister

has her eyes on the apple orchard in your backyard. By mid-September, she'll be on that orchard like ointment on a blister."

"She's welcome to it, if I still own River Ranch by then." His last admission seemed to dampen the conversation. The apple took away any urge to elaborate. By the time he had found its core, Luke had regained his tongue.

"Regarding the waters of marriage, you know you could step right in behind us."

Wray hung his head. He hadn't been able to keep Lacey out of his mind for the life of him. "Maybe my water's too dark and stirred up to drag somebody else into it." He tossed the apple core into an empty cup holder.

"I don't know. Sometimes love has a way of clearing things up."

Wray bit his bottom lip. Rough and parched, he'd make some prize in his current state. He tried to make light of the direction their conversation had turned. "Luke, your head's in a hole in the ground on some backwoods farm in the sticks. That doesn't make you an expert on the ways and wonders of love, does it?"

"Love is the landscape of the heart, Wray. It doesn't have any geography to it and sometimes there isn't any reason to it either. When the time's right, it's right."

"Like harvest dinner, you mean?" He leaned forward to make the turn back toward the grain truck.

"Ease the header bar up. You're about to gobble up the ground." Luke began to repack the cooler with their lunch trash.

Wray mocked a blow with his elbow and Luke

flinched behind the cooler's lid. "You're like a brother already." Though his tone held mock misery, he couldn't hold the grin back as he adjusted the header height in concession.

"Glad to oblige," Luke replied with sincerity as he balanced the cooler on his lap. He rode the rest of the way with his eyes closed, the air conditioning doing its good work all the while. When the auger buzzed out, Luke came to and stood bent-backed, ready to leave. A wave of hot air burst into the cab as he opened the door and stepped out.

A touch sad at losing his companion, Wray wanted to send him off on a positive note. "Hope there's not a line at the elevator."

Luke nodded and started to close the door, but tucked his face into the open crack. "Think about coming on in, Wray, as the getting hitched water sure is fine."

Wray shooed him out, engaged the auger, and watched the grain pour down like gold ore. He wondered how much life he could afford if he were to pay for it one truckload at a time. He tried to shake Lacey's image, but her green eyes kept staring back at him in expectation. Their last kiss floated back to him, hungry and trapped against the doorframe. Maybe there would be a time to set it loose—after the countdown.

~

Lacey perched on the rail of her parents' back deck as the last of the fireworks trickled down onto the surrounding hillside. With the arrival of her intended launching point, she tried to order things in her mind.

Her mother stood and started to load empty glasses onto a plastic tray. "Pretty nice show this year." She nudged her husband's arm. "Hand me your glass, honey."

Lacey studied their interaction and cherished their effortless togetherness. "Mom and Dad, I might be having some fireworks of my own. Anyone interested in the details?"

Her father lowered his glasses. "Aha. You've met someone at work."

"I've met a special someone through work, you could say."

Her mother returned the tray to the table. "Tell us everything," She crossed her arms, her face lit with anticipation.

"Well, I met a young rancher west of town when I went out to deliver a Notice of Default to his family farm. I literally fell into a water trough and he had to fish me out. You can imagine how embarrassed I was, but he came to my rescue and even lent me an over-shirt to cover my wetness while I delivered the official warning for the bank. We ran into each other the following weekend when he helped my friend Julie at a community garage sale. That's when the mutual admiration kicked in and we've been seeing each other all summer. It's actually pretty super."

Her mother stood speechless, but her father beamed with approval. "That sounds amazing, sweetheart. But how's he going to beat the foreclosure? Is his situation gaining ground?"

"Wray's eleven-year-old niece just passed away from leukemia. He had been diverting his mortgage payments to fund her chemo for months. With wheat harvest this week, he should be able to sell the grain and bail out the farm before the end of his foreclosure period. His sister is a widow, and there wasn't any insurance to cover the treatment. Though a heartbreaking situation, things are turning around for the better. I have every confidence that Wray will beat this thing. His parents left him a ton of farm debt when they were killed in a grain elevator accident almost five years ago. He detests the debt and is a hard worker, Dad. And I'm learning so much about farming. I even have a herd of goats that Wray lets me board at his place."

Her mother wrung her hands. "Goats? Oh my word, Lacey. What about your future in banking? You've worked so hard."

"I'm in a special investigation unit right now, Mom. As a matter of fact, we're investigating unusual procedures from our own REO department on Wray's foreclosure case. Because of the conflict of interest in my position, I can't date Wray until the foreclosure clock winds down, but we'll pick up where we left off and make every day count."

He father stood and approached her along the rail. "We haven't seen you this happy in a long time, sweetheart, and that's what really matters to us in the long run."

"Thank you, Dad. Thanks for understanding. This feels like the real thing, as long as I don't mess it up with how the foreclosure is handled. Wray is going through a lot right now, and I want to be there for him, but it's not possible until this situation plays out. I've been his advocate in secret and found some unclaimed resources through their farm insurance and such. If the bank would allow me, I'd do more for our clients' benefit and leave the NOD threats to someone else."

Her mother nodded, sympathetic to her plight. "You never liked that aspect of your work anyway, Lacey. I'm glad the bank is coming around. That shows some sensitivity to a segment of their clientele who could really use it."

"I'm right with you on that one, Mom. So while we're on the subject, I wondered if I could maybe ask you and Dad for access to my wedding fund? I'd like to have the money in my account now, just in case."

"Lacey, that money is yours," her father replied. "We trust you to use it at your own discretion. I can send you that bank check before the end of the week. And when you do use it, there'll be no questions asked and no explanation needed."

"We'd like to be invited to the wedding, of course," her mother added.

Lacey walked over to her and wrapped her in a huge hug. "I may need you both there earlier than the wedding, if this foreclosure thing gets any more complicated. You're my reinforcements."

"Ooh—intrigue. I love intrigue," her father quipped. He held out his arms to be included in the family hug.

Lacey complied, her laugh echoing out into the night to join the sound of freedom.

Chapter 20

Wray hated banks—no, he abhorred them. He loosened his collar as Wren placed her hand on his arm to calm him. He read the placard on the desk and wondered if this could be the same Julie that he'd helped at the garage sale. The smell of fancy perfume hung over the desk and made him even more uneasy. This wasn't exactly how he thought it would end up, but he had come to make his best effort. After full payment of the final hospital bill, the wheat income amounted to less than he'd hoped. Now the end of July, the mortgage had fallen eight months behind. Maybe the bank would settle for a partial payment. They had to try.

Julie slid into her seat in a hurry. "Here we go. Sorry for the delay. I didn't expect you today, so we didn't have your file ready." She looked over her prim glasses at him.

Wray squirmed. The heat of her inspection generated a mild repulsion. The woman he'd met on more casual terms at the garage sale was nowhere to be seen. Maybe that could be attributed to the tables being turned in their current situation, as he now needed the favor.

"I'm the one who insisted Wray come in today," Wren said. "I'm his sister and should be facing the debt situation on the family farm with him."

"Why, that is certainly commendable," Julie replied, "and may I add that I am sorry for your recent loss."

When Wren dipped her chin in acknowledgement, Wray figured nothing more would be said of a personal nature, so he launched right in. "I'm interested to see if I can get the foreclosure clock to stop by making a partial payment today." He was not about to lower himself into deeper negotiation on the loan. Partial payment represented his best offer.

Julie flipped the file open and glanced at the debt roster clipped to the inside cover. She pressed on her adding machine and entered the numbers on the missing mortgage payments.

Wray counted out the eight entries to satisfy himself that her accounting was accurate.

When a total came up, Julie recorded it on the ledger. "Forty thousand, four hundred and twenty dollars," she relayed. "That is the amount that will stop the foreclosure process. How much were you planning to pay today, Wray?"

His throat went dry at the chasm between the two sets of numbers. "I have ninety-five hundred to pay in."

Wren pulled to the edge of her chair to better

address the bank executive. "We had more, but needed to pay the hospital bill for my daughter."

Uncomfortable releasing such personal information, he took a breath and held it.

Julie nodded and seemed almost sensitive to their plight. "All we can do is back it off the total, but a partial payment won't affect the redemption period, I'm sorry to say. Fidelis Bank requires payment in full to stop the default. Would you like to deposit this against your loan debt, or would you like to reconsider your options?"

Wray nodded without flinching. "We'll make the deposit."

"Fine. I'll be glad to handle that for you," Julie replied. "That leaves you twenty-three days to fulfill the balance of the debt. I'll have that total for you once I've taken this deposit to the teller. Give me just a minute." She accepted the check and stood to make the transaction.

Wren stood with her. "Tell me, is Lacey Woodhouse here today? I'd like to see her."

Julie's face turned stone white at the request.

Steam came out from under Wray's collar. He reached for his sister's arm to pull her back under his control but Julie's hand rose in forbearance.

"Our ladies' room is right this way, ma'am. I'm certain you'll find it most accommodating while I arrange for your request. Follow me, please."

Wray caught the slightest wink as Julie turned toward a panel-lined corridor opposite the teller's window. In an instant, he realized Lacey would soon be passing through the lobby to meet with Wren. The impulse to bolt shot through him. Rather than suffer humiliation face to face, he yielded to the more primal instinct and rose to his feet. He found the sidewalk out front in seven easy steps. For his reward, the overhead July sun made him pause and reconsider. The dress shirt he'd selected added insult to injury and he stood there sweating over his pride. He eyed a bronze statue of a little girl feeding ducklings, unaffected by its charm. In twenty-three days, all heck would break loose at River Ranch. How in the world would he stop it?

~

Lacey pushed the heavy-set door and peered into the restroom's interior, not sure who she would find. A slight figure at the sink turned around when the door squeaked, and her heart exploded with happiness when she recognized Wren. They grabbed arms and jumped up and down like little schoolgirls being reunited after an intolerable separation.

Finally, Wren smothered her face into her shoulder and attempted to stifle a raucous laugh. "Lord knows, it's good to see you, Lacey. My world's gone upside down at least twice since I've seen you last. Thank you for your note about Pleasance passing and the pink carnation wreath. That was awfully sweet of you."

Lacey looked her square in the face. "How are you doing, Wren? I mean really and truly. Level with me."

"I just take it a day at a time. That's all I can do. Luke helps me a lot, Lacey. At harvest dinner, he up and popped the question, asking me to marry him." A blush started up the woman's neck and she clamped her hand over her mouth.

Lacey felt like a teenager in the moment. "What did you tell him?"

"You mean after I whooped it up around the table?

I said yes, I would be most delighted to! And he kissed me right there in front of everybody. Wray slapped his back and Joshua tugged my skirt to get a hug. It came as an amazing bright moment after a long tunnel of darkness, let me tell you."

"I'm so happy for you. Is Wray here with you today?"

Several expressions flitted across her friend's face until the last one caused her brow to knit. "That rascal must have skedaddled outside after Julie went to get you. He brought the wheat money in—or what was left of it after the hospital bill. I wanted him to make the first payment because the hospital offered installments, but he insisted on paying it all to spare Luke the entanglement. Of course, that left him short of what he owed on back payments to the farm mortgage, so Julie said the foreclosure clock still keeps on ticking. I don't know where he'll get the rest of the money, and he only has twenty-three days to figure it out."

"Please believe me. I'm helping him in every way possible. But this thing is going to have to run its course, Wren. And it's bound to be hardest on Wray. There's nothing I can do to shelter him right now. But I'll be back out there with him at River Ranch when it's all over, rest assured. Tell him I said to trust what he feels, not necessarily what he sees. That's going to sound contradictory to a man who doesn't pretend."

"Come see me, Lacey. Say that you will. Come by and we can plan the wedding together. I'd really like to hold it at River Ranch right when the apples are ripe. Wouldn't that be a fitting celebration? We could share nature's abundance with our guests."

"I'd love to come out. What day of the week is best

for you? I'll come right after work."

Wren's eyes lit up at the prospect. "Make it Wednesday. Joshua has children's choir practice before service and I'll have the house to myself."

Lacey felt the warmth of heart-bonding friendship like she'd never experienced it before. "Wednesday, two days from now. I can be there around six-thirty. Let me pick up a couple of bridal magazines to give us a head start. What else can I bring?"

Mirth filled her expression. "Not my brother, that's for sure. He's downright skittish regarding the untried waters of matrimony. But Luke is working on him."

Lacey laughed and it echoed against the stalls, so she covered her mouth to stifle her reaction. She put her hands on her friend's shoulders and gave them a squeeze.

"Anything can happen when God wants it that way."

"I have a whole lot of faith in God, but not as much trust in mankind."

"That's because you work at a bank," Wren replied. She touched her cheek and out the door she went, delicate as a bird.

Lacey retreated into a stall with the phrase "untried waters of matrimony" encircling her thoughts. How would she ever concentrate for the rest of the workday?

~

Wray stood looking at what used to be his western fence line. Only the post holes remained, and some of those were already filled in.

The sheriff dug the toe of his boot into a dirt mound where the corner post had been and shrugged his shoulders. "I've been in office for forty-six years,

Wray, and I've never come across anything like this. Now, there have been fences put up where they didn't belong, but never the opposite. All I can do is record it, unless you can point me in a direction of proper inquiry."

It took all of Wray's forbearance not to point at the neighbor's spread up the road, but he didn't have a shred of evidence beyond a hunch. Jumping to conclusions was not on his list of bad habits. "No, I want you to document it, just like all the other times." He stuffed his hands into his pockets. "Guess you wouldn't approve my sitting out here with dad's old shotgun to keep the coyotes out, now would you?"

The sheriff combed his mustache to hide an unauthorized smile. "With the cattle out and your chickens sold, you've got no worries with the fence down, for now. Come next grazing season, it will have to be rectified, for certain."

"I don't have any money for a new fence, Sheriff Earhart."

The older man nodded, his eyes acknowledging the foreclosure situation without a word being exchanged. "Let me try to have a stronger presence in these parts until the end of the month. Isn't that when your redemption period expires?"

"August thirtieth, to the day. I understand you're involved with that in some way."

The sheriff nodded his head and stepped down into the roadside gully to return to his vehicle. "Don't take that personal, Wray. The bank has their expectations and wants them followed to the letter. My job requires the task, whether it turns my stomach or not."

"Join the club," he replied in commiseration. His

perimeter wall had been breached, and now his empire stood open and vulnerable. Why did more hurt always seem to pile onto the already wounded? He stepped into the sheriff's truck for a ride back to the house, his mind further numbed by every added complication.

~

"Not quaint enough." Wren flipped to the next page in the bridal magazine. "Too much flesh showing. Why is everything strapless and gut hugging?"

Lacey giggled and turned to a page she had folded down. "Consider something like this." She traced the lines of the skirt with her fingertip. "Imagine this one with some straps or sleeves added to the bodice. You shouldn't worry about a form-fitting dress. You've really kept your figure, Wren."

"Thank you, but I don't want anybody's eyeballs falling out of their heads on account of my dress. Look around, we're in 'modest town' here."

"But you had considered holding the wedding up at River Ranch, right?"

"Do you think it could work out? Even after the foreclosure deadline, I mean?"

"Something tells me that the new owners—if there are new owners—would be most open to having your wedding on-site."

"Ah, I used to lay up there in the hayloft and dream of dressing up like a bride."

"We could make that dream come true and use the loft as your dressing room before the wedding. That would be so incredible—the ultimate chic nook experience…"

"And the men could be waiting for us down below. Wouldn't that be something? Luke wants to ride his horse up the aisle. I think that would be spectacular. My heart races when I think about it."

"Okay, then think about where the altar would be in this dream. How about centered under the elm tree? We wouldn't even need a trellis. We could tie some tulle and drape it from the branches."

"That sounds really beautiful, Lacey. And it would give us a shady spot in case it's hot that day. We've settled on the fifteenth of September. That's the second Saturday of the month. Luke wanted to give Wray some time to adjust in case he has to leave the premises."

"How very thoughtful. I know Luke is raring to get this union started, which makes his gesture all the more endearing. You're getting a good one, Wren."

"Don't I know it. You are going to be my maid of honor, aren't you? I don't have a soul to stand up for me except you, Lacey."

"I'll be there no matter what, I promise you, even if your brother doesn't cooperate."

"He's standing up for Luke, so he's participating even if he's not cooperating. He's in a funk again. It's the fence. This time it's been taken up lock, stock and barrel."

Lacey stared at her, not trusting herself to even open her mouth. Her cheeks burned before she could manage a breath.

"Hon, you're red as a beet. Don't let that bank do your insides like that. I'd turn and walk right away— that's what I'd do." Wren scrunched her nose up and flipped the magazine page. She covered the model's revealing neckline with two fingers across the page.

Lacey paused to give her reaction some thought, as it had never occurred to her that resigning could be a viable option. She could add that to her growing list of things to pray about, right after her petition for a new place to live.

Chapter 21

Wray stood in the background as the hopeful bidders took the prime spots on the courthouse steps by the auctioneer. Sheriff Earhart tipped his hat as he went by, acknowledging his presence at the sorriest gathering west of the Mississippi River. Despite two more payments to the bank, he had not been able to raise the total necessary to keep River Ranch from foreclosure. This would stand as a day of infamy for the Benson clan, a soul-stabbing defeat he wouldn't forget for the rest of his life.

Footsteps came up behind him. "Sorry to hear about the ranch, Wray," a man said.

He turned to find his western neighbor standing there with a bid number in his hand. "I bet you are, Darold." He hooked his hands into his pockets for safekeeping. A middle-aged couple arrived and approached the auctioneer's table to register. Darold tipped his top-of-the-line cowboy hat and retreated to less hostile environs.

Somehow, the people didn't seem to matter to him anymore, as he shrank into a kernel of misery. What others saw today represented a cardboard cutout of who Wray Benson used to be. A has-been, he'd become a washed-up rancher who had failed to keep the family farm together. He had the sudden urge to get sick right there on the courthouse steps, which would have added another dimension of unpleasantness to the grab bag of assorted memories for the day.

"Mr. Benson, you didn't have to come out, but it's good to see you again," Julie said as she stepped up beside him.

He glanced over her shoulder and saw several more of the team from Fidelis Bank, including Lacey, who stood off the front of a black car beside a taller man. A bald man signaled to Julie and walked up to join the auctioneer behind the table. "Looks like all the powers that be are assuming their positions for the annihilation of my ancestral lands." Like the cardboard cutout he had become, he found it impossible to move.

Julie pressed the toes of her shoes up to a sidewalk crack, taking great care to place them evenly. "Not everything is what it seems today," she replied. She let her sincere gaze linger a long second and turned to join her associates.

"And some things are worse than they seem," he replied, his voice sharp with acrimony. His gaze trailed over to Lacey. There she stood, propped up in her red high heels, just like the first time he'd seen her. His heart tried to tell him something, but the rest of him wasn't in the mood. In fact, he kind of liked this hollow drum feeling. He thought he could get used to it.

In minutes, the auctioneer cackled like a

chanticleer from the top step and individuals began raising their numbers in odd synchrony. Darold Henley's hand went up every other bid, it seemed. No big surprise there. Wray conceded that the farm would likely go to him in the end. After all, he'd already done his fence work to meld the two half-sections together. His gaze drifted to the sheriff, who stood by like a wind-up soldier, allowing the process to play out with a tin heart of indifference. His father had thought a lot of the good sheriff back in his day. How wrong can a man truly be?

With his volume turned up a notch, the auctioneer rounded what sounded like the final corner. The late-arriving couple bid one more time, but Henley quickly countered it. As silence lingered, he held his number in the air like a victory signal. A gavel struck the table and the word "sold" pierced the air. His neighbor, now his successor, approached the table with his bid number leading the way while the brief murmur died and the divestiture fell complete.

Wray stood alone toward the back. "Well, that was relatively painless for ninety-nine percent of our attendees."

"I'm more concerned about the one percent," Lacey replied in passing. "Don't stop watching now, as it's about to get real interesting."

He caught the way her calves flexed with every step, but would not allow it to affect him, though halting the reaction proved difficult. The bald man approached her with a scalding tone, but she held her rigid stance, unwilling to play along. The man left her and went to consort with Darold Henley at the auctioneer's table where they were both promptly met by the sheriff. Heated words began to fly in the exchange, but Wray stood too far away to overhear the specifics. He followed Lacey's advice and kept watching.

Henley began to throw an all-out fit. He pounded the auctioneer's table with his fists.

Wray's eyebrow shot up and his stoicism cracked, as he had not anticipated such an unchecked demonstration. The sheriff placed a hand on the winning bidder's shoulder, and before Wray could draw a breath, he twisted the man's right arm back and threw half a set of handcuffs on it. The man's expensive cowboy hat flew off in the ensuing scuffle, but the sheriff expended superior strength and the matching wrist soon found the cuffs. With a shove, the sheriff brought Darold toward his car, attempting to load the farmer into the back seat.

Wray unfolded his arms and felt the circulation seeping back into his core. Some convoluted act of justice had unfolded right before his eyes. If he hadn't been such a quitter, maybe he could have picked up on the clues sooner.

Next, the bald man hastily cut a bee-line toward the banker's car. Lacey ran down the courthouse steps and only made it two truck lengths before she blew out on her high heels.

A trickle of nervous heat ran down the back of his neck, putting him on high alert. Before Wray could blink, Lacey had yanked one shoe off and threw it down the strike zone at the escaping man. When it made connection with a loud pop between his shoulder blades, he shrieked but kept running.

"Stop him, Wray!" Lacey called, her tone

desperate.

His numbed countenance caught fire in the moment. In two anticipatory steps, he extended an arm and clotheslined the passing escapee which knocked him to the ground. Wray shoved a boot against the middle of his back. The squirmy conquest brought a sense of satisfaction out of nowhere.

"Be glad to take him from here, Wray." The sheriff huffed between words, winded from his run over. He jerked the second culprit up off the concrete and clamped on the handcuffs. "Much obliged." A smile curled under his graying moustache.

Lacey hobbled up to retrieve her shoe. "Wray, please meet Harold Odom, my former boss at the bank and your neighbor's half-brother." The man leered at him before the sheriff yanked him away for a family reunion of sorts.

Wray's mouth fell open as the taller dignified man came and took Lacey by the elbow as soon as she got her shoe reattached. When she glanced back longingly, he felt another quadrant of his interior thaw out. Just as he had arrived, he once again stood alone.

~

The past two weeks had flown by for Lacey, a strange mingling of bank details, house paint and flowing chiffon. She entered the farmhouse sunroom and examined the expanse of space offered by the removal of forty years of furniture accumulation. The sheriff had delivered the note from her parents to Wray that graciously informed him they were the new owners. They asked him to vacate the house for renovation, as per Lacey's plan, and allowed him to keep his possessions in the barn with the farm implements. Wren contributed a diversion by having her brother work on her house in Yoder to fix it up for resale.

Lacey entered the kitchen and scrutinized the new coat of light gray paint, then tugged at the multi-colored valance covering the window above the sink. She had a hundred plates spinning in the air, and any one of them could come crashing down at any time, but if it all came together today as she planned, it would be totally worth it.

"Dad thinks he's finished with the rabbit hutches and wants to know what to tackle next, Lacey," her mother called.

She pulled a checklist from her pocket and swiped her hair back. "Have him add that bottom rung on the hayloft ladder next, please. Then he might need to get cleaned up for your trip to the airport to pick up the girls."

"Sounds like a plan. I hope this feels like it's coming together, honey. The house looks incredible. I love every improvement you've made."

"Thanks, Mom. I would say it's starting to feel a little more like home, but there's one too many unknowns for me to be that comfortable." She turned and her gaze fell onto the stained glass meadow hanging across the sunroom windows.

"Wray will appreciate it, Lacey—because he loves you. Men have a reluctance to see their world in a new light, so give him every opportunity. And stop your worrying."

She drew a deep breath and glanced out into the farmyard where the elm's shadow had shrunk with the advancing sun. Adrenalin shot through her veins and she jumped off the kitchen floor. "Let's keep the ball rolling then." She stashed the first fruit tray in the refrigerator. "Did the caterer call to confirm?"

"Check. And I'll do the floral pick-up after we leave the airport."

"No matter how the day turns out, Mom, I'm glad you're here."

"I wouldn't miss this for the world, honey. Think positive now."

Lacey offered a hug and they filed outside to tackle the next thing on the list together.

~

Wray tossed his saddle into the back of his truck. "Not a bad day for a wedding." He raised the brim of his hat as the sun shifted higher in the cloudless sky.

Luke followed suit with a sheepish grin on his face. His saddle thumped onto the truck bed. "Here's a nugget of gold for you, my friend. Remember those chicken coops over there and how we'd play house in them as kids every time you guys came out?"

"Like it was yesterday. In fact, Josh's new pony looks a lot like the one you used to let me skedaddle around on."

"Well, here's the tip I want you to mull over today. At some point, every cowpoke needs to give up his gallivanting ways, get off his pony and settle into playing house."

Wray blinked and shifted his saddle blanket to better pad the saddle during his ride to the ranch. "You're the one getting hitched today. I'm just an innocent bystander. But I'm more than ready to see Wren happy again. I can't say enough about what that means to me."

Luke shook his head and gazed out on the horizon past the corral. "Don't you think she wants as much for you, Wray? This farm foreclosure hasn't been easy for her, either. But she wants you to shake off the mud from being so low, and stand up again. The Benson name flows through your veins now." Luke reached in to polish the silver trim on his saddle with his cuff.

"And I've managed to let it be wiped off the map."

"Something tells me they haven't printed the new plat maps yet. I'm just asking you to stay open to what this day brings as a gentleman's promise and a handshake between near brothers." Luke turned and shoved his hand toward him.

Wray fought the urge to turn away once again from a difficult life challenge. Something overrode his apprehensions, and before he knew it, his hand was in Luke's to accept the challenge.

"Now I'm holding you to it."

Luke's sincerity cracked a window open for genuine feeling, and Wray allowed a little sunlight to penetrate his rode-hard-and-put-up-wet existence. "Let's get the horses loaded. If I'm gauging the time of day by the sun's heat correctly, it's half past prenuptial preening and a quarter to hitch-up time.

Luke chuckled. "Yeah, Wren will have my neck if I mess this day up."

Wray clasped a hand on the neck of his brother-in-law to be and steered him toward the barn.

~

Lacey peered down from the hayloft opening. "The guests are here." A charter bus opened its doors and out stepped a multitude of quaintly attired guests from the village of Yoder, partly enticed by her offer of an apple harvest after the wedding ceremony.

Wren ran her hands down the cascading satin of her dress. "How do I look?"

Lacey stepped toward her with her hand on her chin as she studied every aspect of her ensemble. She reached to anchor a hair comb deeper into the crown of her wavy brown hair, which straightened the short veil tucked behind.

"You look stunning, Wren. Luke is going to choke when he sees you. It shows just enough skin to let him know what a lucky man he is." She gazed into her friend's eyes and shared the moment of unabashed expectation with her.

Wren folded her hands against her chest. "Lord, please let him know some of that already."

A wave of appreciation washed over Lacey as she held the bride's shoulders and felt her tremble.

"And I pray that for my brother, too, Lord. That Wray could look at Lacey in the unblemished light of love."

"That's sweet of you, Wren, but today is your day, first and foremost. God will truly have to shed his grace on the rest of our plan."

Wren nodded to the coat rack nearby. "I'll be here for you."

Lacey hugged her and smelled the rose water on her skin. "I know you will, like the sister I've always wanted, here in the nick of time." She swallowed a lump in her throat and blinked back a tear. "I'll have to trust God for the rest."

Wren looked up with a twinkle in her eyes. "Remember our pact? No crying for the women folk today."

"Right, we'll let the men cry. Now let me carry your jacket down."

Wren crossed the loft with a rustle of satin. "I'm always gonna love this place."

Lacey unhooked the jacket's hanger and glanced around the humble chic nook. There, next to Wren's nature tokens, sat her dried daisy bouquet, the driftwood souvenir from that day on the river, as well a stem of buttonbush, with its ball-shaped seedpods that hung like a promise still longing to be fulfilled. "Me too, sister." She halted at the top rung of the ladder to conduct a final heart check before facing the men.

~

Wray glanced over at the dark coats of the Mennonite men, and it came to him how odd his father might have found the day, since the village had finally come to them in a pivot of destiny. The four o'clock sun burned as hot as mid-September allowed, and Luke sat ready in the saddle for his ride up the aisle. Wray's awareness seemed to operate in slow motion as he took in an unreal world. He had been in this barnyard a million times, so why did it seem so new on this particular occasion? He dropped his stirrup and mounted, a best man runner-up if ever there was one.

Music cued their arrival, and Luke spurred his horse forward out of hiding, cornering the barn with little excess. Wray tried to mimic Luke's lead and speed as identically as he could. Once abreast of the back row of guests, the rhythm of being on horseback helped settle his jagged nerves. While Luke nodded to his acquaintances, loose and at ease, Wray rode rigid under their inspection. Before he became aware of the aisle's end, Luke had stopped. He reined in too late, bumping against the lead horse's rump close to the altar. He pulled back on the reins, glanced down in recovery, and found Lacey just off his left stirrup. His gaze froze on her gorgeous frame. When her eyebrow arched to welcome him, his chest caught on fire.

A man on the front row chortled at his riding blunder. Wray accepted Luke's reins as the groom dismounted, and reined right to get into position. A young groomsman appeared to take the horses as rehearsed, then Wray dismounted. In a few steps he found himself on the front line at the altar while pinpricks of heat needled him from every angle. When Luke turned toward the preacher, a vision of happiness, Wray became acutely aware that the pain was all his.

A fully bearded minister stepped in front of the couple. "Who gives this woman to be married this day?"

After Wren shot him a suggestive glance, Wray cleared his throat for the response. "The honor belongs to both the Bontrager and the Benson families."

Wren turned back to the minister, looking satisfied.

A victim of position, Wray still couldn't shake the feeling that all eyes remained on him. Blood suffused his cheeks and he resisted the urge to bolt right out from under the elm all the way to the river. After an exaggerated blink for clarity, he turned his head and Lacey filled his center of vision. Like a saint whispering vespers over those who couldn't help themselves, her lovely lips moved in prayer.

Out of the fog of all his loss and divestment, a remembrance came from the inner recesses of his soul. The minister repeated an ancient scripture about the depth of love, as Lacey continued her private petition.

When she appeared to be done praying, he read her lips to see if she pronounced the "amen." The benediction never came. Why did that strike him as hopeful? The elm lent its shade and he began to get comfortable up on the front line, a real miracle.

Chapter 22

Lacey thought the dinner fare had turned out memorable and gave kudos to the catering staff as they cleared the buffet line and pulled back inside the house. Members of their Sunday school class had arrived in time to be served, and Wray seemed to be having a high time in their company. Too bad he hadn't taken five seconds out of his day to say something to her.

As she walked back toward the banquet table to signal Luke, she became introspective. Had she been overly presumptuous about the continuation of their relationship to the point of delusion about how the day might end? A girl could get her hopes up but what happened after reality came crashing down around the dream? A recovery site developed, that's what, complete with wounded victims and the turn away of the indifferent. She cleared her throat as her cousins approached, and endured the supportive hugs they wrapped around her.

"How's the forecast looking for the grand finale?" Gwen, the oldest asked.

"Wray is truly amazing, Lacey," Lynn gushed.

"I think he's going to come through for you," Bren predicted.

Lacey's lip trembled as she thought of the right thing to say. Honesty could be blunt at times. "Well, let's just say that it might help if he would bother talking to me. Even a word. Anything. This silent treatment is becoming a dagger in the back, if you don't mind me saying so. Anyway, I have to get the after-dinner toasts going, but I don't think it's going to loosen his tongue. He probably doesn't have a toast planned, knowing Wray."

"Go get 'em, girl," Gwen replied as she walked away.

Lacey shot a thumbs-up behind her but knew she needed more than luck. A breath-prayer eased out as she stood behind the women's side of the table, facing Luke. She mouthed, "It's time," and stepped back to her seat.

Luke clanged his fork against his water glass and stood to take the lead. Wray rose with him, a glass held in one hand while he loosened his tie with the other. Luke smiled and gave way, sitting back by his bride.

Lacey refilled her water goblet and couldn't contain the unease that shot like a steam bank up her neck.

"To my sister Wren and my new brother Luke—thank you from the bottom of my heart for reminding us what happiness can be like. To tell you the truth, I'd almost forgotten, but God has been good to us this day. May every blessing he has for you amble up your path."

Lacey raised her glass and clinked with several guests, her palms sweaty at having to speak next. To her surprise, the bride stood and looked down the table.

"I'm claiming the next turn," Wren teased, full of grace. "Most of you might wonder at the refiner's fire this family has been through to reach the pinnacle of this day, but some of the mystery of our turn around must be revealed right now. God has been trying to get our attention, yet many might view the loss of loved ones too harsh a tactic for a loving God. Regrettably, we Bensons are a hardheaded lot, so we suffer. But God in his redemptive plan has strewn our path with some wonderful, loving people to shine some light on the way out."

When her voice quivered with the admission, Luke reached a hand out and took hers.

Wren gave it a squeeze and looked up. "Let me talk about River Ranch a minute, as maybe that will be easier to express. Many of you don't know that my brother, Wray, paid for every last treatment that Pleasance needed in her fight against the disease that finally took her from us. In doing so, he put his land in jeopardy with Dad's inadvertent load of debt, as his mortgage payments went instead to pay for medicine for a period of more than eight months. I'd like to publicly thank him for such sacrifice. Wray, without you, she wouldn't have had any chance at all…" She made a sweeping gesture from her heart toward him.

Lacey could barely look up, feeling unworthy and a touch self-centered all of a sudden. A general commotion caught her attention and when she peeked, the Mennonite men had stood and began to give Wray a rousing ovation. After she recognized several men from the livestock auction, she faltered. When the impulse struck, she pushed back from the table with a knee-jerk reaction to run like the wind. The maid-of-honor dress gave her cause for concern, as its satiny sheath had not been made for speed and durability. She quelled the reaction for the moment.

~

Clarity focused Wray's mind as validation from the Mennonite community settled around him. Wren held her position at the head of the table, and his anticipation soared at what would come next. His gaze shifted to Lacey and she looked like a restless hostage with invisible bonds.

"The foreclosure clamped down like a vise with the summer's heat, and Luke came up to help Wray harvest a fine crop of wheat, the profits applied to the balance owed. But it was not enough. Only God knew that the foreclosing bank would begin to struggle at the same time as ours, uncovering a rotten scheme inside the REO unit. That's when the foreclosure took something more precious away from Wray, as Lacey Woodhouse opted to courageously step away from River Ranch to root out the evil preying on the bank's foreclosure victims, Wray included."

A murmur rose from the men's side of the table as the comforting hand of Wray's Sunday school teacher slid onto his shoulder. He glanced at Lacey, who looked like a deer trapped in a thicket.

"So this toast is for Lacey, my maid-of-honor and much, much more. Through her advocacy for the downtrodden, she not only recorded the fraud within the bank, she exposed the collusion of a neighboring rancher and something more, which I am now happy to reveal. Lacey single handedly approached the insurance company regarding our losses at the grain elevator explosion and secured almost fifty thousand dollars in settlement claims for the equipment losses, plus five thousand more from the Mennonite Relief Fund to offset our parents' burial expenses. Wray, all that money waits for you in an interest-bearing account at Fidelis Bank."

Something intangible shifted off of Wray that had been there since the day his parents had been taken away—the burden of debt. He took a breath and sensed freedom.

"Due to a technicality of the property being under lien and the bank's desire to have the foreclosure run its full course for the criminal case against the perpetrators, none of that money could be used to redeem River Ranch. So Lacey acted on the last day to make the redemption payment and halt the foreclosure herself. I understand from her parents that the money was set aside as her wedding fund, but she unselfishly employed it for what she held as a higher cause."

Wray loosened his collar as he began to choke at her last admission. He looked at Lacey, but she was out of reach, like a white-winged dove poised to take wing. When he glanced back at his sister, she had a document envelope in her hands.

"Under my authorization as a Benson, I've asked the bank to apply some of the money Lacey uncovered to pay off the remaining debt. It is my full honor to now present the title of this working ranch to my dearest brother, Wray Benson, as a testament to his tireless devotion to our family."

He stood to accept her envelope, rallied by the

thunderous applause of their guests. In the well-wishing that ensued, he lost track of Lacey until he saw a figure running away under the elm tree. Elders from the Mennonite community led the guests in an old-fashioned hero's tribute and their hip-hip-hurrah echoed between him and the barn where she had disappeared in haste.

Joy slipped to worry as guilt riddled its way through his mind. He flashed a solitary finger across the table to Wren and excused himself toward the barn. The guests settled into murmurs of mirth as he heard Wren explain that he needed a minute of privacy. The men chortled collectively which jangled against his eardrums. He rounded the barn door and soon spotted her satiny shoes abandoned at the base of the loft ladder.

"Lacey? We need to talk…"

"Don't you dare come up here after ignoring me all day."

He climbed up three rungs at a time, set on having the confrontation and getting it settled. "Listen. I believe I owe you at least one apology and several more thank-you sentiments." When his head surfaced above the hay, she threw an ancient wasp nest at him. "Let's talk about this rationally, can we?"

Lacey sobbed, backed further into the chic nook, and searched for her next weapon.

He recognized the selected piece of driftwood from their canoe outing. With a hand in the air requesting peace, he advanced up the ladder.

"Tell you the truth—I don't feel like being rational anymore." She let the weathered root fly with some fairly impressive force.

Exposed to waist height, he took the blow across his forearm. It made him wince. Okay, now they were both in a little pain. "Look, blame me for the disconnection. I blame myself, quite honestly." Determined to be off the ladder, he eased up and stepped onto the loft. With the depth of her fury heating things up, he peeled off his jacket and left it hooked on the ladder.

"Great. You're to blame. Finally something we can both agree on." She turned and groped the dusty shelves for her next projectile.

"While you went to battle for me, I shut down in my misery. Nothing was the same for me after Pleasance died. I couldn't pull out of the tailspin." He swallowed hard, his gaze bearing down on her as he stepped closer.

She picked up a turtle shell and hoisted it, threatening to let go. "You couldn't trust me that things would work out? Two months and then we were going to pick right up again, remember?"

Her words scorched as they seared their way into his heart until a slight motion distracted him. He squinted to make sure he was seeing this right. A shadow had started on her right wrist and now moved up her forearm at a snail's pace. Heaven help him, she was in such a fury she hadn't even noticed. But he knew she would soon enough—and it would be a hideous scene. Moved to protect her at all cost, a renewed confidence of heart shattered his passivity and birthed a yearning from deep within to protect her.

"Lacey, do what I say. Drop the turtle shell. Spiders are crawling out of it." On impulse, he maneuvered the first rapid step toward her.

She launched the missile and caught sight of the arachnid assault in one fluid motion. Cavitations began to wrack her shoulders as she let out a piercing scream. The fire in her eyes turned to chilled fear.

Wray ducked the shell and lunged for her frame. His first attempts to wipe the repulsive culprits into the hay only partially worked as she thrashed against him, wild-eyed. He glimpsed a sheet hanging nearby and snatched it toward them. He wiped her flailing wrist until convinced he had scraped the trespassers into oblivion. He held her there pinned against him until the phobic reaction waned to a more controlled sensibility.

Lacey sobbed as a final shudder worked through her body.

"Wray? Is everything okay?" Wren called from below. "We heard the scream."

He caressed Lacey with his gaze and puffed back some loose tendrils of her hair. Tender proximity spoke a message all its own.

Tears flowed from the corners of her eyes as the fear departed and became replaced by something sweeter.

"Spider attack, Wren. She's phobic. I've got it under control now, I think. Give us a minute or so to collect ourselves…"

"I'll give you ten minutes, and then the cake cutting will transpire. That's Lacey's Plan B by the way, which I'm not as fond of big brother. I thought Luke told you to get off the pony. If you have the courage to, Elder Glazner needs signatures on your paperwork."

He glanced over the hayloft rail and saw her stomp out of the barn below. What caught his gaze next, he didn't expect. There on a coat rack where the sheet had rested hung a wedding dress with embroidered daisies swirled across the front. Plan A stood in front of him as the hopeful second bride wiggled to squeeze out of containment. Instead of taking offense as the last one to know, it landed as the most sincere compliment he'd ever received.

"You're not going anywhere until we settle this, bow-stroker." He made the tease extra soft and personable. His eyes raked her features in as she heaved for breath in her satin sheath. A fire kindled in his chest, making him grateful to be in a superior position. "Was I going to be the last one invited to the second hitch-up this evening?"

"If you had checked in with me earlier, a hint of it might have come your way sooner." Her long eyelashes fluttered into a moist blink.

He took it all in up close and extremely personal, as physical rebirth became part of his redemption. What a remarkable, breath-drawing feel it had to it. "Don't make me wait one more second." By his last word, his lips were on hers in a place of yielded forgiveness that grew to dazzling pleasure. From his prisoner grip on her wrists, his fingers slid into hers and her resistance dissolved into cooperation—and plenty of it.

"Now marry me and make me the happiest man on earth," he whispered in her ear.

"I will—and I fully intend to," she replied, with a promise hidden in her tone.

His kiss to seal the deal came softer and less hurried, as he had everything he wanted right here in the hayloft.

She finally wriggled out from under him with a

giggle. "You get down that ladder and tell Luke it's back to Plan A." She pulled some straw from her hair.

He unclipped the jeweled clamp that held her up-do and her black hair cascaded around her shoulders in shiny waves. He smiled his approval and backed toward the ladder. "Now you're talking, bow-stroker. I like where this boat is heading."

"Send Wren up and I'll meet you at the orchard," she replied.

He grabbed the jacket and let it ride on his shoulder as he slid down the ladder fireman style on his way to his own emergency. The ground under his feet welcomed him back. His mind raced to come up with a way to let Lacey know she'd redeemed more than the ranch. His old parade move of a fancy side pass gait rose to the top of his options and he slapped his hands together with approval. He could hardly wait to tell Luke to get back on his horse.

~

Lights twinkled as Lacey stood, front and center, under the foremost tree of the apple orchard. Wren stood by her side along with the three cousins, all looking down the aisle of spectators awaiting the men by horseback. Little Joshua rode in first on his pony, its mane platted with sunflower-tucked braids. Luke came down next and stopped to take the tiny box of rings from his new son. Their horses were escorted off to the corral and Luke stopped to kiss Wren before he took the opposite side to wait for the groom. The pause gave Lacey a moment to collect her wits and she whispered a prayer into the top of her buttonbush bouquet. Surely Wray would come in and save her at long last. Her knees grew weaker by the second.

In the interval, she wondered if it had been enough, all the days of separation, her endless quests to learn how to manage a farm, the nights searching for missing money to which he was entitled. The whole frenzy of entangled thoughts knotted together in an attempt to lend her the worth she needed to stand up here and become his bride.

Suddenly Wray appeared at the end of the aisle, sitting straight-postured and beaming his affection toward her. At the top of the aisle, he made the horse turn and approach sideways, working its way in some fancy cross-step that gave him a jaunt in the saddle with each step. The back row of Mennonite guests began to applaud the purposeful showmanship and it rippled through the entire audience. Wray smiled and lifted his hat as though to acknowledge he had returned to life abundant. All the while, he never took his eyes off of her.

She touched a daisy on her dress and realized that this must be what true redemption feels like, a selfless gift returned to the heart as sheer joy. A breeze blew and the sweet scent of ripe apples became part of her wedding day memories.

Epilogue

Lacey searched for Wray and found him giving her father instructions up by his truck. Her dad disappeared as the coachman called for Luke. Wren hooked her arm around her groom and hauled him to the carriage as their guests laughed in a circle around them. Luke tucked her onto the running board and Wren took the bench behind the driver. In one eager leap, Luke joined her inside.

Lacey found it hard to hold down the giddy feeling in her chest. Wray stepped up and swept her into his arms. The on-lookers cheered. Birdseed flew across the carriage as twilight snuffed out the day. She ducked against him and kissed his neck as he set her inside. She rested against the tufted leather seats and waved farewell to her family. Once Wray made his way inside, the coachman cracked the reins and the team pulled free of the barnyard.

Somehow, she couldn't get close enough to Wray and when she shouldered into his side, he lifted her onto his lap almost as if he could read her every thought. The sheer hem of her sundress floated over his boot tops and she gave a final wave as the orchard shrank out of sight. In the rush of changing out of her dress, she'd given him the gift of ginger lotion and it seemed that he'd already found it in a few spots, which made her giggle.

Luke pressed the lantern on and a soft light filled the carriage.

"I'll remember this day more than all others as long as I live," Wren said dreamily.

Luke touched her nose with his and couldn't stop grinning from ear to ear.

Wray pulled Lacey to his chest. "Where are you two headed?"

"Some castle on the river in downtown Wichita," Luke replied. "It's supposed to be romantic, according to the brochure."

Lacey could feel Wray's laugh coming before he released it, her hand braced on his chest.

"Our coachman has a car waiting at the end of the road," Luke said.

"You two enjoy the whole ride, because we're bailing out at the bridge," Wray replied.

Surprise leapt in her stomach because, in all her attention to detail, Lacey hadn't given a single thought to life immediately after the "I do." She collapsed against the seat. "What about our honeymoon?"

"All taken care of, little wife of mine." His thumb found the fold of her elbow and made a tiny circle of heat that radiated up her arm.

Excitement of the unknown rippled up with it and she found herself giddy with anticipation. When a charter bus passed the carriage, they all offered a round of waves as the Mennonites returned to their village under the cloak of night, heavy with apples. A steady stream of cars followed. Some blinked their headlights instead of honking horns, to not spook the team of horses.

"You were some sight coming up that aisle, big brother," Wren said. Her words seemed to trail into the night air. "I never thought I'd live to see the day."

He patted Lacey's arm. "It seemed a long time coming."

Lacey sat up and let him close his arms around her as she watched the lantern light sway in his eyes to the rhythm of the horses.

Wray tightened his grip on her waist. "Maybe I should have given up and foreclosed earlier on."

The insinuation wasn't lost on her, and she closed the distance between them, which led to a lingering kiss.

The coachman soon reined back the team. "We're at the bridge, sir."

When the carriage lurched to a halt, all Lacey could see were the railings along the bridge below.

Wray plucked the light source from its post. "We'll take the lantern, little brother."

The coachman held the door open and offered Lacey a hand down. She paused with one foot on the running board and glanced back at her groom. "Where are you taking me, Wray?" She blocked the way down and waited for an answer.

"I'm finally taking you down to the river, just like I promised you that first day," he replied. He stepped down and his free hand found the curve of her hip.

"Your dad brought the canoe over for me and left my truck a bridge or two down the way."

Her cheeks heated as she stepped onto the bridge and listened for the river's subtle voice. The carriage pulled away with a squeak, as they stood side by side along the rail.

"I've got the bow," she said as he brushed against her shoulder. "You steer. And no splashing the happy bride."

A sturdy arm locked around her waist and somewhere from the inky tree line an owl called across the night. Wray nuzzled closer. "I wouldn't dare dream of it." With that promise, he lowered the lantern to highlight the captivating beauty of the river flowing by.

The End

ABOUT THE AUTHOR

Cindy M. Amos writes contemporary and historical inspirational fiction in natural settings to combine her background in field ecology with her Christian walk of faith. Her books weave nature's intricate beauty with humanity's spiritual relevance into seamless plot-driven romance stories with up-lifting, God-honoring endings. A full-time freelance writer with numerous national magazine publications, Ms. Amos has placed as a finalist in the American Christian Fiction Writers' Genesis and Mid-America Romance Authors' Fiction from the Heartland contests. She serves as the south central Kansas chapter secretary for ACFW and writes from Wichita, Kansas where she shares a home with her aviation industry husband and two come-and-go college-aged sons. With the expanse of the tallgrass prairie hers to wander, she loves to name the wildflowers in bloom and has a fondness for the badger on the pond dam.

~Envir-Romance… where love lingers on the landscape~